Anne Marshall, 25, lives 90 percent of her life in the pages of books, whether that's writing on them or reading them. The other 10 percent? Living in reality with her husband and cat, Jillian. She loves writing in the ever-expanding world of fantasy. Every twist, turn, cliffhanger, and deeply written plotline draws her under the waves of the drama and angst that comes along with writing and reading it.

For Kayla

Anne Marshall

THE CURSED PRINCE

AUSTIN MACAULEY PUBLISHERS™

LONDON · CAMBRIDGE · NEW YORK · SHARJAH

A CIP catalogue record for this title is available from the British Library.

ISBN 9781787102941 (Paperback)
ISBN 9781787102958 (E-Book)

www.austinmacauley.com

First Published (2018)
Austin Macauley Publishers Ltd
25 Canada Square
Canary Wharf
London
E14 5LQ

Table of Contents

Bookworm

Looking along the large bookshelf, I ran my finger over each and every spine trying to find the perfect one. I had read every single book in this room and now needed to find a new one. Ending on the last book I huffed, I wasn't going to find anything in this room to read, I needed to go to the bookstore in town. I thought about what I needed to do for the day and tried to plan out when I could actually go to the bookstore. I think I could squeeze it in before I went to school.

I left the office and made my way downstairs when a large explosion stopped me in my tracks.

I rushed down the rest of the stairs and slammed my palm on the kitchen door making it swing open. Entering the kitchen that was now consumed by a cloud of gray smoke, I searched for the source of the explosion. I started feeling around for the kitchen island that would lead me to the counter, which would take me to the source of the explosion.

Hearing coughing, I looked around for the person responsible, I knew it had to be my sister at the other end of this smoke cloud. Fanning my hands around, trying to get a clear view on the situation and listening to the coughs of my sister wasn't helping anything. Feeling around for the kitchen fan I finally found it; flipping the switch and watching all the smoke go somewhere else, luckily the windows had been opened before she started whatever this was. I saw my sister sitting on the floor practically coughing up a lung. I reached down to help her back up to her feet.

She patted herself down and wiped her brow, I wondered what she was cooking up in here that would make such a large blast and so much smoke.

My sister was an experimenter for lack of better words when it came to cooking food. She loved experimenting with anything from food to robotics, robotics being her real passion; she was sort of all over the place. She and I had lived together for the last five years without our parents. Circumstances made us move out a little early.

She looked at me with smoke covered cheeks and started laughing. "Oh god, I'm sorry Henri, I didn't mean to blow up the kitchen. I'll clean up, you need to get to school." She waved a hand around and reached for the broom and rag to start on the cleaning.

I smiled at her and quickly grabbed my bag and headed for the door.

Almost slamming the door behind me, I made my way towards the sidewalk and to the bookstore. I knew I only had a half an hour until I actually needed to be at school.

Walking down the sidewalk heading towards the middle of the town where the bookstore would be, I started humming a familiar tune in my head. Getting lost in the song playing around my brain, I almost didn't realize I was about to walk into someone.

Stopping myself before the collision, I looked up to see the smirk of Gregory Rice. I took a deep breath and closed my eyes; I didn't want to be stopped by him this morning. The incident in the kitchen that Olivia caused made me a tad behind schedule which of course meant that I would run into him. He had been making crude passes at me since we moved here and I hated it, he would also make fun of the fact that I had an American accent and that I still hadn't assimilated into their slang and world. Plus, I really didn't like him.

He didn't know what the word NO meant and it was infuriating. Of course, if I told anyone but my sister about it they would just say, 'Oh, he likes you or, you're such a lucky girl,' I don't know which one made my blood boil more.

Before he could say anything, I sidestepped away from him and kept my walking pace. I didn't stop to look back when he called my name, and I didn't stop when I heard his footsteps catch up to me. I needed to get to the bookstore and then class, that's all I kept telling myself.

Keeping my pace wasn't working because he and his long legs had caught up to me. He grabbed me by the shoulder and forced me to turn around. Looking up at him, I saw his winning smile, the blond hair all the girls fell over and of course, the bright blue eyes that put some of the Earth's oceans to shame. Maybe, if his whole personality was different I might swoon over him like so many others do, but alas, he was an ass hole and I wanted no part of him. "And where do you think you're going? Let me walk you to class, it's the least you could let me do since you obviously ignored me earlier. You broke my heart." He put his hands to his heart and gave me a sad face. *Yeah right.* "Sorry Gregory! I need to go somewhere before school, now if you don't let me go, I'm going to be late. Mend your own broken heart." With my last words, I walked away from him and quickened my pace towards the bookstore, the rubber soles of my sneakers squeaking as I did.

Finally making it to the store, I grabbed the door knob and pushed my way in, I took in the smell of the old and new books that surrounded me. The smell of paper, ink, and binding glue, it was truly the best smell in the world. Hearing the bell from the door ding to sound my arrival, I knew the book shop owner would show herself soon. Until then, I started up and down the rows of books trying to find something.

Hearing the shop owner clear her throat, I turned around swiftly. I smiled when her warm eyes hit mine, she was a good friend of my sister and me; she was the first person we met when we moved here. I had only been twelve at the time and my sister was just barely eighteen. She didn't question why we were on our own or why we chose here of all places to live, she just gave us warm hugs and books.

She knew everything about the town and had probably read every book in the world twice, or so she said. I always came to her for books; her store was packed with them. The space of the book store was small but when you have floor-to-ceiling sized bookshelves and every nook and cranny filled in with books, you find that there is more room than if she had two buildings. They were in an array of colors and textures, some leather, most were hard or paperback but there were a few that had special bindings and she only lent those to me; other people had to buy them. "What brings you here, Henrietta? Need a new book?"

She always knew what kind of book I would like reading and most, if not all, of my books at home had come from her store. "Yeah, I'm out of things to read at home and I need something to get me through the weekend. Olivia is doing a lot of work on something secret and it's causing the house to explode nearly daily since she can't focus on cooking anything properly. Boarding myself in my room for the weekend might be safest." I walked up to the counter and watched her turn around and look through the pile of books that had just come in.

I knew this store like the back of my hand and she had always kept the new arrivals behind her until she sorted them and put them on shelves. Hearing a book fall and a small curse from her, I decided to keep my laugh to myself.

She was always nice to Olivia and me, but she did have a temper. And we both shared a hatred for Gregory Rice. He had vandalized her store once or twice in the past and she'd never forgiven him, plus she knew how he antagonized me almost daily. She was like the weird aunt we never wanted but somehow ended up having, and it turned out to be a great thing. "Here we are, this is a work of fiction and it's actually based on a legend in this town. It's about the cursed prince. Some say it's more than legend and I have my doubts about it, but it is a good read regardless. I'll trade you for the book in your hands now." She gave me a wild smile and I saw that look in her eye. The book in my hands had come from our old home and it was one she had yet to get her hands on. I had read it a million and one times and wasn't too sad to part with it. Even if I was, I could always get it back. "Thanks Margaret, I have to get to school but I'll stop by later this week!" I waved to her after we made the swap and started towards the school. Looking the new book over, I felt the spine with my finger and traced the gold lettering on the cover of the book. *The Cursed Prince*, I hoped it would prove to be a good read.

Tall Tale

Listening to the teacher drone on and on about math made me want to stick my pencil through my eye. I hated math and it wasn't just because it was one of my worse subjects, I just hated the way it made my head hurt. Luckily, it was my last class for the day; unluckily, Gregory was in the same class.

I kept ignoring his whispers and egging on for me to turn around and talk to him. Eventually, he gave up and flirted with the girl next to him instead. Rolling my eyes and attempting to focus on the problem on the board, my mind decided to drift off to the book I just got from Margaret.

The book that Margaret had traded me was on my mind. I wanted to know more about this cursed prince, and what it had to do with this town. I also wanted to know why she said it was a work of fiction if it was technically based off a story in this town. Maybe, whoever wrote it didn't have the entire story? Wishing for the bell to ring which of course, it didn't, I looked back down to the problem I was currently doing.

The loud bell overhead sounded off letting us know we were dismissed from school for the day. I nearly jumped for joy but decided gathering all my things first would be smarter. Quickly putting books and notepads into my backpack I saw a shadow fall over me.

Not needing to look up to see who was standing over my crouched body, I let them know I wasn't interested. "Go away, Gregory, I don't need to be walked home from school. Thanks." I finished with the last book and zipped up my bag. Carefully standing up, making sure I made no contact with the brick wall named Gregory in front of me; I got up from my desk and started for the door. "Why won't you let me do anything for you? All the girls in this school want me, why don't you? I'm the hottest guy you will ever meet. Don't turn away from me and pretend I don't exist, it's not right." I turned back for a moment before I exited the classroom and gave him a glare. "First of all, looks are not the only thing in the world. Second, I'm glad everyone else wants you, go stalk them. Third, for it not to be right would imply that I have been outright rude to you or mean in the slightest when I have been nothing but polite and have told you time and time again that I'm not interested. Take the massive hint Greg and leave me alone. Goodbye." I waved my hand in his face and made my way to the hall, wanting nothing more than to get the hell out of there.

On the walk back home, I sifted through my bag and brought up the new book I had traded for. Running my hands over the cover again, I noted that it was warmer this time from being in my backpack and hands most of the day. I cracked the book open and read the first page after I got past the title pages. Its dedication was to the curse breaker, which I found a bit odd, but I assumed it was part of the story.

Starting the first page I began reading:

As the legend goes, the prince of the land was a nasty and cruel boy, he only thought about himself and how to get what he wanted. His father did not want to give the crown to him and instead thought it wise to teach him a lesson.

He called upon a powerful witch from the nearby woods and ignored the rumors that surrounded her. He paid her a great deal to put a curse on the boy, nothing too serious, and something that would scare him into thinking of others. He wanted his son to be generous, loving, kind and a great king. He told all this to the witch.

What he did not know was that the witch had met the boy before and had been met with the same crudeness she was now hired to scare out of him; she knew better. Instead of scaring him, she decided to go a different way; she wanted him to have a fate worse than death.

When the king gave the witch a key to his room so that she could do the job she was hired for, she greedily took it and began her plan.

She walked into his room as he lay sleeping and while being as quiet as she could, she restrained his limbs to the bed.

She made sure that he could not move an inch and when he woke up as she did the last restraint, he screamed and yelled for help. Knowing that the king would not send anyone in, she continued with her work.

She brought a sack of liquid from her bag and after she pried the prince's jaw open, she dumped the whole thing into his mouth. He was forced to swallow the foul liquid she had given him and when all of it was ingested, she let him go. Smiling at his grimacing face she brought the dagger out of her bag. "Cruel and evil boy shall be what his heart shows. You shall live with this curse until another shows your heart a new path, but be forewarned, if you do not find the curse breaker when the sands of time run out than the cursed shall live in anguish and misery for the rest of eternity."

With her last word, she plunged the dagger into the heart of the prince, ceasing his mortal life.

I closed the book when I noticed I had walked all the way home. I knew that book would be good but to start out like that, this would be interesting.

I looked around the hills and far off fields for signs of the legend come true. I looked upon the remains of the old castle, the one that was practically falling down around the edges and the one the story is supposed to be about, and I thought about what this town was like all those years ago. But instead, I walked up to the door of our house and grabbed my house key.

Just as I was about to walk through the door, something quick and bright caught the corner of my eye. I looked back over the fields and hills and then to the castle. Something so far away wouldn't have caught my attention, so why did I find myself looking at the castle and its windows? There hasn't been a monarchy for this region in nearly a century and I knew no one lived there… maybe it was just the light of the sun catching me off guard.

Irrefutable Offer

Accidentally slamming the door closed, I made my way to the kitchen. Seeing and smelling that the smoke had cleared out of here made me feel at ease. I loved that my sister experimented and made new things out of old ones but sometimes it got to be a bother. Walking around the kitchen I found a note sitting on the counter. Picking it up and reading what my sister had left for me, I sighed.

I had forgotten she would be gone for a week starting today. This was a regular occurrence and I was used to it, being alone in the house for a week wasn't that big of a deal. Plus, I would have a better time with the quiet I was so longing for.

I trashed the note and grabbed something cold from the fridge to drink. Finding we had orange juice, I jumped at the chance to drink some. Usually, my sister took the orange juice with her to work but this time she left it.

I poured a glass and put the jug of OJ back into the fridge. Walking to the living room with my new book in hand, I slung my backpack down to the floor and flopped onto the couch and started surfing the TV channels in hopes that there was something on this time of day. I was lucky that she had fixed the TV before she left too; usually she used it for parts in one of her experiments.

Taking a long drink of the juice, I fixated myself on a channel and began the mind numbing lazy Friday afternoon I had been waiting for.

Not long after I started my relaxation did the doorbell ring. I groaned and set my juice on the small table in front of me. I sort of wished I just stayed on the couch and pretended no one was there, but even I can't be that rude. I got to the door and opened it with more force than needed. Seeing the older man at my door left me confused and no, I was just confused. "Can I help you?" I asked the statue man. "Yes, does Henrietta Black live at this residence?"

I was skeptical about him, no one ever used our last names, and even we barely used them. It was our mother's maiden name. I had never seen him before and if he was working for my parents, which wasn't a far stretch, then I didn't want him to know who I really was. But if he just needed to deliver something then I wanted it. He didn't look like a delivery boy, man, whatever. He wore a clean-cut suit and had a kind but stern face; he seemed more like a butler than an errand boy. "What business do you have with her?" I tried to sound professional and probably failed miserably at it. "I have documents explaining that she has come into possession of some property; we have finally been able to nail down the bloodline that the property belongs to and it fell to her, but if she isn't here then I will return another day." He started to turn around, but I stopped him, I wanted to know more. "I'm Henrietta; sorry for pulling your leg, I was just… never mind. You said you found that I own property here? There must be a mistake; I'm not even from here. My sister and I came from America and have only been here for about five years, I can't have any property that's been handed down to me." The suit looked at me and pulled a large manila envelope out of his suit jacket and handed it to me. It was heavy with lots of papers and I wondered if this was all a big joke or something. "The documents tell you where the property is, how much it's worth and what your options are; the main reason we found you instead of your sister is that you are the last Black family member that can hold property. Your sister owns this house and we thought it best for her if we locked you into this property. We couldn't get a hold of your parents and then it fell to you, it's been in your family since the 1700s, back when this town was run by the Cross monarchy. The envelope explains the rest, good day." I looked at the envelope and before I looked back up he was gone, odd.

I closed the door and walked towards the couch with the rather large envelope in my hands. I studied it and before I opened it I made sure the TV was still on, I liked the background noise. I picked at the small metal clasp that held the lip of the envelope down and when I finally got into the paper, I pulled out a rather thick set of documents.

I thumbed through everything and read to myself some, glancing over the whole thing and trying to get the gist of what that man was offering me. I mean, I never in my life thought our family actually came from here at one point. It would be completely coincidental that we ended up living here.

The top page had this family crest on it and the more I squinted to see the details of it, the more I saw that it looked familiar. I'd seen this on a couple of my mother's things. I guess we weren't adopted like I had hoped, because this looked like our family crest, the one I never knew about. To find it again in the UK of all places was even more odd, I mean I was Asian for crying out loud and so was our mother, our father was white but that's the wrong side of the family tree.

I read the part about the family ties and it stated that when the royal family was alive and flourishing, that the Blacks were the royal guards and that they protected the King, Queen and Prince with their lives. It went back generations and the top guard for the royal family had always been a Black. I guess, that was interesting. The big question was, why would the guard's family end up owning the property? Why not the people that owned it before, like the generations of people that came from the king and queen? Did something happen that killed the line? These were all good questions but the other biggest one was, what the hell was I going to do with a freaking castle?

Yeah! That was the property, the old castle on the hill. The castle I just happened to be reading a book about and then this man showed up and told me that it's mine now. This had to be some sort of exhaustion induced dream.

I continued to go over the papers in my hands and saw the different options. I could sell it, which would be a hassle. I could live in it, which would be nice, but I bet it needed a lot of work and that wasn't something I would do. The last option was to demolish it, but I didn't know if I could handle tearing down something that had been there since the 1600s, or even older than that. I needed to check this place out and decide from there. Maybe, if I put off reading the rest of these papers I could actually enjoy my weekend and do the rest of this on Monday. Until then, there was no reason Olivia needed to know about this, maybe it would be resolved before she got back. Until then, the TV was calling my name.

A Wicked Boy

Waking up with a large envelope lying on my chest and the new book lying on my legs, was not how I usually woke up; I usually was buried underneath an entire stack of books, not just one. I gently sat up and looked over at the TV that I fell asleep in front of and turned it off. Getting off the couch and heading to the kitchen for something to drink, before I went upstairs to shower and finish reading over the large stack of papers the weird guy yesterday gave to me.

I gathered the book and the papers in my hands while I balanced a bottle of juice in my arms with everything else. I took the stairs one at a time since I didn't want to drop anything. Pushing my bedroom door open with my hip, I stumbled into my room. Throwing the book and papers onto the bed, I got ready for my shower.

Taking a quick shower, I got out and started drying out my hair with a towel and then throwing it into the basket and flopping down on the bed; wearing nothing but my robe. I laid on my stomach and went over the papers in front of me, combing through every little detail that could get in the way. All that it was showing me was that I now owned the castle on the hill and that it was, in fact, not a dream I was having. I owned a freaking castle!

The place was updated back in the late 1800s to the early 1900s so there was running water and most of the pipes were still in good shape, so it says. It didn't say if it had gas going through there, so if I needed to clean up before I sold it, if that's the way I was going to go, then I would need to find that information out. All of this being dropped on my lap was making my head hurt, but maybe this was what my life needed? Maybe this was a sign that my life was going to get interesting again.

I got to the last page of the paperwork and found the line to sign my name to the deed of the castle, I wanted to sign it, and it was a contract, I would just figure out what I'll do with it later; I just needed to find a pen. I got up and slipped on a pair of jammie pants and a thin shirt, so I didn't get too hot during the night. I looked around forever for a pen and when I finally found one, it didn't have a cap on it. *Great!* I only hoped it wasn't dried out.

Finding the last paper again, I brought it over to a harder surface so that I could sign it properly. Nearly having to dig into the paper more than necessary because of the dryness the pen was giving me, I carefully signed my name and put all the papers back into the envelope. I followed the directions listed on the third page and put the entire manila envelope into our mailbox and flipped the red flag up on the side.

He didn't specify if I should put a stamp on it or anything, or a return address so I assumed they would find it themselves. I shrugged my shoulders and walked back into the house to read a little before I did anything else today.

I walked the hallway back to my room and made the short turn through my doorway and over to my bed. I flopped back down onto the covers and grabbed the book from my pillow, cracking the book open to the first chapter. The prologue of the book was how the prince was cursed, but the first chapter of the book started with his childhood.

I started with the page in front of me:

While the prince was wicked when he was a teenager and set to take the crown, he was a completely different person when he was a child. When the prince was born, the whole town celebrated for three days, everyone loved the little prince. His mother, the queen, was completely in love with the small child, she carried him in her arms always. The king was even drawn to his magnetic personality, even if he was only a few days old.

The new prince had bought a mist of happiness around the kingdom and its people, and for the first six years of his life that happy mist stayed over them.

After his mother passed away due to her own grief, the prince began to act out. The king mourned for his queen and when he retreated from his son, the prince only got worse. He would run wild through the streets of the town and cause mayhem in his wake. As he got older, the mischief only got worse. When his father bought him in on a punishment for a town's person that had broken a law, when he was thirteen, and the king finally saw what a monster his son had become.

When the king asked the prince to hand down the ruling for the man who had broken a law, he assumed he would say something like a month behind the bars. But what the prince had said in front of the law breaker had shocked the king to his core. The king had also known that since he gave him permission to rule down on the law breaker, he would have no veto power. 'As the crown prince, I decree that this man be stoned and caned to death.' The words had left the prince's lips before the king was able to prevent the guards from taking the law breaker and doing what the prince had told them to. He thought that giving him the power for just a day would allow him to see what being a king was really about, but he was power mad, and that was never a good sign for someone that would be the king in a few years.

He blamed himself, he kept saying that he should have been next to him to stop his decree but since he wasn't, the guards took his decree and had the man stoned and caned until he died a slow and painful death. But even if he had been next to him, he would have no power. It was traditional in their family that when the prince was of certain age, he would have a full day of being the king so that he knew what to expect when the crown was passed to him. His father before him had done the same thing, and when it happens the current king has the same amount of power the prince would have and vice versa.

From that day on, the king kept an eye on his son and he only got worse. The king made sure that the prince was never in that much power again and the only hope running through his mind was that he could help his son before he passed, otherwise he would have to destroy the royal family, and their monarchy would cease to exist.

I read the chapter over and over, making sure I really understood where the prince was coming from, but I couldn't find a reason behind putting a simple law breaker to death. This guy was truly evil and there was still more of the book to read. I closed it for the day and thought about the story and how it seemed to linger in my mind. There was something more to this and I knew it, I couldn't shake an eerie feeling that I felt when I thought about seeing the inside of the castle on the hill.

Fairy Dust

Sunday had come and gone, even school Monday morning went by rather quick. It was like the universe was telling me to get my butt to the castle doors to start the process of checking the new castle I just inherited. I left the school and ran home quickly to get the stuff I had put together last night, and then I was on my way to the castle. I figured I would need cleaning supplies and some snack to hold me over until I left for the house again.

It didn't take as long as I thought it would to get to the castle doors. It also helped that I rode my scooter here too, with all my supplies on the back of it, of course.

I looked up at the giant door that seemed to be staring me down. Shaking the feeling of being an ant, I put down one of the buckets of cleaning products, brooms and other various brushes I might need depending on the condition of the castle.

I pulled the large skeleton key from my jean pocket that I had found in the mail box yesterday, in place of the envelope I had put in there on Saturday. I looked at the keyhole and the doorknob that connected to it. It was weird to see a door this large had a knob and keyhole this small. I slipped the key into the hole and felt the metal make contact. Turning it to the left a bit and finding it only resisted, I tried going to the right and when I felt the tell-tale click of the pins in the lock, I put the other bucket of cleaning products down and turned the knob with my other hand.

The giant door groaned when it was opened for what I could only assume was the first time in a hundred, or so, years.

I let the door stay open while I grabbed the two buckets and waddled in through the doorway with them. Every step I took into the castle made more and more dust loosen and fly into the air. I could barely see anything with all the curtains closed and

26

the fact that there was no working electricity or lights. I was happy that I remembered to bring matches with me and the more I thought about it, the more my sister's extra portable generator might help more than I thought.

I dropped everything from my hands and stood in awe of the dust covered room. I was sure it was amazing without all this grime all over it. Maybe keeping it would be a good idea, who knew what I could actually do with this place.

I did a total 360 degree turn around the room and looked at all the nooks and crannies that the room had to offer. I couldn't see much since the windows were covered except for a few, which made the fact that I had thought I saw something up here the other day all the odder. Since this was technically my castle now, I thought about snooping before I got down to business; I needed to make sure there wasn't any trap doors or anything of course.

Walking through the large room that was most likely the foyer, I trailed down the hall that was off the room and into yet another room. This one looked very similar to the last one only different furniture, maybe another foyer? I guess it could be considered a study room, or like the room you take your guest to after dessert to drink coffee. I never understood that, why drink coffee after eating all that food? *Rich people.*

I followed the next hallway to what I could only assume was the dining room and what a room it was! The long, and I mean long, wooden table was covered with a thin white sheet and then with a few layers of dust. If it weren't so dark in here with the curtains being closed, then I would probably be able to see the paintings on the walls and the different decorations.

I walked over to a pair of curtains and ran my hand up one, grabbing the side's edge, I pulled the one side over and found that it was much heavier than I had anticipated. Using both hands to pull the one side all the way open and then switching to the next making sure they were both fully open, and the sun was shining through the very dusty glass.

I walked back to the table and as I did, my feet kicked up the dust that was even covering the floor beneath me. I turned back to see the light hitting the dust cloud that was rising from the floor into the sun lit air. The particles looked like fairy dust.

I was happy that dust didn't set off any sort of allergies because walking through the cloud that was floating in the light I knew I got it all over me. I patted myself and walked to the next room. Somehow, finding my way into the kitchen which was probably the dirtiest room of the whole place, I inched around the kitchen island and the just plain nasty. There were pots and pans in the sink, some hanging from the ceiling. At least those were clean. The newer updates show that they were placed under a faucet in the kitchen; it was basically a tube coming from the wall and over the sink. I would have to pump the water from the well pump next to the counter.

So, since I was now responsible for this place, I was going to have to clean it no matter what choice I made in the end. I would probably have to throw the dirty ones away. No way was I getting century old food off of pans. I wasn't ready to dive into that mess. I left the kitchen in its state and found myself at a set of stairs.

I followed the flight and as I kicked more and more dust up into the air, I reached the top of the staircase. I took a right and walked down the hall of doors, not really wanting to explore those right now. This place was pretty boring for a decrepit castle that used to host balls and royalty from different parts of the world. Maybe, if I could actually get it cleaned enough, some of the magic would come back.

Turning around and starting down the other hallway, I found nothing but more and more rooms. Deciding that I would choose one at random to investigate, I stopped at the last door on my right and grabbed the door knob.

The cool metal that had a thinner amount of dust on it, I turned it, wanting to know more about this specific room for some reason. When the door opened, I was met with a weird site; another staircase. Only this one went down through the floor and the wall, it was really out of place. It was an odd place to have a staircase going down through the wall next to it. I walked into the room and followed the stairs, seeing that it went into the wall next to the door and down into some sort of castle abyss.

Was I curious enough to go down a mysterious staircase that seemingly led to nowhere? *Yeah! I was.*

I started on the staircase and walked down the creaky steps and when I had to crouch under the wall to get to the rest of the staircase other than that it was a normal way to go down a set of stairs. The whole way down was dark and eerie, but I kept at it. It wasn't the scariest thing I'd ever done. Plus, I picked up a candle stick from the wall before I made my way down and lit it to light my way down the staircase.

I got to the bottom of the stairs and the more I looked around, the more I realized I was in the basement. I didn't think that the stairs went that far down. Why didn't they just make a case going down to the basement from one of the several rooms that were used for entertainment? Instead, they wasted a perfectly good bedroom.

The basement was cold and dreary; I didn't like basements, the movies always pulled them off as somewhere the murderer hides his bodies, or cuts them up, or even where all the ghosts live. I brushed all the movie scenarios off my back and stepped further into the basement. I came across what I had been seeing nothing but in this place; more doors.

It was like this place was made of them, or something. Every door looked the same and when I finally got to the one at the end, I stopped and looked at it. It was iron as opposed to the other wooden doors. I stared at it in the dim lighting and I could have almost sworn, there were traces of silver in the metal. I traced the smooth surface with a single finger and found it to be clean; for once something in this place didn't have any fairy dust on it.

I shrugged my shoulders and turned away from the door, when a small sound hit my ear. I stopped. I turned back to the door and wondered if there was some sort of mouse, or rat trapped in there. I wanted to open the door and see but when I reached for the key in my pocket and put it through the keyhole, it wouldn't budge. I guessed the rat would just die off on its own; hopefully it wouldn't get out and scare me when I was looking around the rest of the castle.

This was a skeleton key; it was supposed to unlock everything. Wonder what was really behind the ironclad, silver-spotted door in the basement?

Boom Box

With all the exploring I did, needless to say, I didn't do much else on Monday. So here I was Tuesday, already tired from a long day at school, cleaning a castle that I may or may not keep, I mean it really is too big for my sister and me and I didn't know of anyone who would sell it or would buy it. Maybe, I could get it protected by the town so that it wouldn't get knocked down or anything. I had decided that starting on ground zero of the filth would probably be the best thing. So, I lugged all the cleaning supplies and all the brooms, even the generator for the vacuum I had brought so it would make things easier; I lugged it all to the kitchen. I really didn't want to do this room, but I knew that if I kept putting it off, I would never get to it and I really wanted to see what this place looked like clean before I made my decision. Plus, I was going to ask my sister what she thought too.

Shuffling around for a decently clean spot to sit my stereo before I got started was a hard thing to do. Every inch of this massive kitchen was covered in some sort of gunk, be it dust or grime from the past.

Finding a spot that seemed to only be covered in dust, I put the stereo down and made sure the batteries were well in their holder in the back of it. I clicked the 'on' button and tuned it to a local station that I had grown to like. I turned the volume up and as the music began to pump through the speakers, I turned to my cleaning supplies. I grabbed a trash bag and the can I needed to throw it all into and started throwing the dishes and pans that I knew would never be clean again in there.

After a while I was in a groove, cleaning and dusting, sweeping and even getting down on my hands and knees with a scrub brush, making sure the floors sparkled. I made sure all the counters were cleaned off before I started on the floors. I looked at my watch for the tenth time that day and realized it was nearly eleven at night. I didn't think I would get lost in cleaning like that but when you're doing it to music, time seems to speed up.

Throwing the dirty rags in the sink and collecting all the cleaning supplies so that they were nice and neat when I came back tomorrow, I needed to get out of there and get some sleep. I had been cleaning for nearly seven hours, and I had to say this kitchen looked amazing. If I wasn't so curious to see the place in its prime, then I wouldn't be cleaning so much.

From the ceiling to the corners of the floors, there wasn't a speck of dirt to be found. My sister and I had a knack for cleaning and cleaning really well, we learned it from living with our parents and cleaning their messes up. I had gotten used to cleaning our house from top to bottom, especially when I was stressed out, it helped me clear things out of my head while I cleaned things around me. Olivia was just as tidy except when it came to her experiments, she tended to be extra messy, and I usually stayed away.

I swept the area with my eyes right before I left for the front door, making sure the stereo was off before I did as well. Heading for the door, I stopped right before I grabbed the door knob. Listening for just a moment, I could have sworn I heard music playing again. Not wanting the batteries to die just in case I didn't turn it off, I went back and checked on the stereo.

Finding that the stereo in the kitchen was fine and completely turned off, I headed for the door one last time hoping I wouldn't hear a sound.

I made my way out of the castle and when the night air hit me, a chill ran up my spine. I didn't think it was going to get down this low tonight, I should have brought a jacket. I hugged my arms to my body and made my way towards my scooter.

I swung my leg over the seat and sat down on the black leather. Tilting the scooter to the upright position, I put the key in the ignition and started it up. I loved my scooter, it was bumble bee yellow and went fast. I only used it for long distance; I didn't need to use it to go to the bookstore or school, unless I had a lot of things to bring home. But since the castle was up the trail and then up a large hill, I knew I would need my scooter.

I strapped my helmet to my head and clicked the buckle in place. Revving the engine, a bit, I picked my foot up and then started down the hill on my scooter. Once I had some momentum, I picked my other foot off the ground and made my way down to my house.

Chaining my scooter to the side bar, I had near the garage and then heading inside the house I wondered about the sound I heard before I left the castle. I looked up at the daunting shadow of a castle before I went inside the house completely. Squinting my eyes, I looked closer at the upstairs bedroom windows. I could have sworn I saw the shadow of a man, but that would be ridiculous. My sight wasn't so great this far away, but I knew what I saw, and I ignored it anyways.

I shook off the silly thoughts of someone actually living in a place like that for hundreds of years; sometimes my imagination got the best of me and I needed to reign that in. That book I was reading must have been giving me crazy thoughts.

Hearing the bell ring throughout the school was probably the best sound that could ever happen. It was the end of the day and I was actually wanting to go back to the castle to clean up some more. I had hoped no one noticed me going up to the castle because I didn't want to explain the weird news I had gotten this weekend.

Stuffing some books into my locker and making sure I had my current book in my hands before my walk home, I slammed the metal door and headed for the exit. Parting the book's pages, I started bouncing from chapter to chapter, I was a quick reader and I knew that if I missed something I could go back and read it again. Plus, this book was set up strangely. It didn't help that I took a day, or two in between reading the different parts and chapters so it seemed like I read slower than I really did.

It started with who and how the prince was cursed, then it went on to tell about him before he was a menace, and now I was on the chapter about what his father had done after the witch cursed him. I wasn't complaining, it was a good book after all.

The king had found out what the witch had really done to his son and needless to say he was not happy about it. He knew that if he didn't put his son away that the curse, he had been dealt, would consume him and the town below. He was doing it for the good of his people.

He had read in an old book that trapping someone with a curse, as his was, in an iron room with as much silver as possible would prevent the cursed from escaping. So that's what the king did.

Under strict secrecy he had his metal workers construct a room in the basement next to the rest of the prison rooms. This room would be iron clad, even the door and its hinges would be made of iron. But the special part of it was that he told them to mix in as much silver as they could get their hands on. Making sure that when he trapped his son down there, he would not be able to get back out.

His metal workers thought he was mad for doing this, but they didn't dare question their king. They went to work making the special room and they even put in a secret staircase in the old prince's nursery, something no one would find easily.

When they had finished, the king himself looked it over and when he was happy, he paid his men handsomely for their work and their discretion. While his cursed son slept one morning, he took the herbs that the witch had given him to make sure he wouldn't wake up in the middle of being taken into custody.

His guards had taken and put the prince in the specially made room, locking it for the rest of his life. From that day on there was a guard stationed outside the room, and since that day the princes always tried to trick the guard into letting him out so that he could get his revenge. His father thought ahead and made sure that his best man was on the job, and only allowing the generations of his family after that to be the guards.

The king regretted asking the witch to curse his son, he only wanted him to be scared straight. And now, when he passed so too would the monarchy his family built.

I closed the book when I realized I was at my house already. I looked back at the path I took home and wondered how I got through the traffic of the town without looking up a single time or being yelled at. This book was really capturing me.

When it spoke about the room they trapped the prince in, I thought about the door I came across the other day. It was iron and silver, just the thing the king would have needed to trap him. If I could find the key, I would really be able to find out the truth. Margaret did say the book was based on a tale from this town, there was an old castle on a hill, maybe this was more than a story after all, and I couldn't ignore the similarities anymore.

The Prince's Keeper

I laid on my bed with the moon shining through the window and bathing my bed in its silvery light. I couldn't sleep, it was one in the morning and I just couldn't get to sleep. Something was nudging at the back of my mind. I threw the covers off my body and quickly stood up. I needed to clear my head and the only thing that would do it: juice and television.

I walked to the kitchen and grabbed a bottle of juice, taking it into the living room and flipping the television on, I turned to the channel I needed for this to work. I walked to the back of the TV and checked the cords, making sure they were in place. When I heard the sound of static coming from the screen in front of me, I knew it would be any moment.

I waited, and waited, and then like a channel flipping on, my sister's face appeared on the screen.

I watched her fiddle with the camera and then go take a seat in front of it. Her long black hair was flipped over her shoulder as she straightened her shirt before she began.

"Henrietta, this video is for you when you need it. Maybe I'm out of town and you can't sleep, maybe you had a nightmare and didn't want to wake me up like usual, the reason doesn't matter, just watch this message and know that you are safe. You are loved and that nothing bad will ever happen to you.

"I know that our past is scary and that it keeps you up sometimes, and that sometimes it gives you nightmares and I'm so sorry about that, Henny, but it's over, it's behind us and we will never go back. Perhaps I should tell you the story that I used to when you were younger."

Her voice filled the room and my mind, there was nothing like hearing her voice to make me feel safe. I love my sister and I know she sacrificed so much when she took us away, she did it out of love and for our safety. I tried to push back the memories of our old lives, but they were being dredged up again. I turned the volume up and listened to the story she would tell me before bed when I was younger.

"There once was a brave knight that roamed the land on their mighty steed, making sure all the boys and girls of the town were safe and sound in their beds. This knight was a special person you see, because they not only protected the people of the town, but they protected the prince from his nightmares.

The knight would stand guard outside the prince's room and made sure no harm came to him while he slept, but what he didn't know was that the danger was inside the prince's head. When the knight found this out, he would tell the prince magical stories about happy and wonderful things before he went to sleep and after that day the prince wouldn't have a single nightmare. The knight saved the day once again.

But as the prince got older and bad things began to happen, the knight had to guard the prince from more than just bad dreams and bad people; the knight had to guard the prince from himself. You see the prince's father, the king, punished the prince for doing something unfitting; a prince of his age and the knight was told to guard the prince until the day he died, making sure he did no harm to himself, or the people down below. And ever since the knight guarded the prince, the town and he had been safe and sound."

She ended the story and smiled at the camera, after wishing me better dreams, she ended the tape and the TV went back to being static. I had heard that story since I was five years old, way before we moved to this town and before I traded Margaret for that book, but the stories were so similar.

I got up off the couch, forgetting about my juice and anything else I had gotten out before. I swiftly walked to my room and opened my bedroom door. I spotted the book right away on my night stand. I quickly walked to the book and cracked it open, letting it fall to the chapter I needed.

Previously, I had just glanced at this chapter telling myself that I would go back to it later. But I needed it now.

I skimmed through some of the words I didn't need and landed on the ones I did:

After the king had the prince sentenced to a cursed life in the iron prison cell, the prince began to plot how he would escape. He had never felt this angry towards his father before and he knew it would only fuel the curse. After waking up to his skin burning off his bones and watching new skin take its place, and after having his teeth fall out only to be replaced with sharp knife-like points did he want everyone in that town dead, including the witch who did this to him. The curse made him crazy and he had no relief from it, it would pound in his head relentlessly.

He was in immense pain and he couldn't shake it, when he thought his body was starting to get used to the pain, a new sensation would hit him and create a new feeling of pain and anguish. There was no rest for him.

He couldn't eat the food he once loved, and now only craved the life force of the people around him. He wanted their blood and wouldn't stop thinking about it, until he had a drink. His father had sent him blood of animals that had been hunted for the town but that wasn't enough. He needed human blood. The screams and wails could be heard throughout the castle and after a while, most of the staff left the king to be alone with what he had created.

Stories were told about the prince going mad and trying to kill people and they were not farfetched, since some of the screams could be heard down the hill. The people in the town below were scared but the king assured them that he was locked up and would be no trouble to anyone.

The prince had not let up a single day with his screams of pain and the king was beginning to go mad with its sound. He sent his best knight down there to calm him down. The prince knew the knight well, since he was the one that kept him out of trouble when he was younger. He was fond of the knight and hoped that this would be his way out. The knight knew better.

The knight would stand guard outside of the iron and silver door, despite the pleas and screams for him to open the door. The knight knew he just wanted to kill everyone. After years of guarding the prince, the knight began to grow old and tired, so he sent his son to be the new guard, and after a while it stayed like that. When one knight died they sent for the next generation and so on.

This continued until the last of the knights had been born, the stories say that there are still family members from that very line out there and since the prince stays unguarded in the castle, it's just a matter of time before he finally gets the freedom he's been screaming for.

I closed the book and thought back to the story my sister had always told me. Once when I asked where she had heard it, she told me that our mother told it to her when she was my age and her father told her the same story and it went along her father's line since the late 1700s. Now it made sense, the story of the Prince's keeper is a child's version of The Cursed Prince.

We were a part of the knight's family tree, and it had to be on my mother's side because that's where I heard the story first and that's where my sister had gotten it from. The story has been following me and now I was supposed to pick up where the last knight left off. Maybe I was crazy, and the lack of sleep was making me think insane things. I couldn't be a knight, I just couldn't be.

The Iron and Silver Door

I had to do it, I had to know the truth behind the legend, but where to start? I quickly shuffled around my room and grabbed some clothes; I wasn't going to wait until the morning. Even if I had to skip school for the day, I was going to, I was a decent student and I worked hard when I needed to; I hadn't missed a day since we moved here. *They wouldn't miss me for just one, right?*

I grabbed a bag and stuffed some other supplies in it and walked to the back of my closet. If someone were to walk into my room, they would see that it was a normal teenage room; messy. But if they were to go into my closet, they would see a disaster area that really should be quarantined for the safety of the whole town. It didn't help that I never cleaned it, I really should hire someone else to clean the castle.

I shuffled through my things and moved old shoe boxes around on my shelves, looking for a flashlight. I knew I had those battery powered lanterns still there, but I wanted something smaller for the basement. Something I can slip into my pocket or hold with my mouth if I need both hands for whatever reasons. With all this clutter, I wasn't sure where I started out in here and where I just ended.

Moving the last box, I found my old blue flashlight rolling around on the top shelve, I stretched up and grabbed it only to knock another box onto the floor. Hearing a more than loud drop for an empty box, I got curious and bent down to see what was inside. Prying the lid off and trying not to choke on the dust that was now dancing in the air, I felt around in the box for whatever was weighing the box down and making it thump to the ground. My fingers met something cold and metal; not remembering what I left in the box I pulled it out of there and held it in my hand.

When I looked in my hand I saw that it was an old key, similar to the skeleton key I had for the castle doors. This one seemed different somehow, like it wasn't metal at all. It wasn't as heavy as the other key that was most likely made of iron, this one was much shinier and smoother; maybe it was silver? I didn't know they would make keys out of silver, depending on when this key was actually made. I decided to pocket the key and made my way out of the closet. Maybe, this was the answer I had been looking for.

Not wanting to waste any more time, I quickly left my house. Making sure the door was locked, I got on my scooter and left for the castle.

The front door seemed to glare at me this time around. I had only been in the castle a couple of times, but this time felt completely different. The weight of the seemingly silver key was heavy in my pocket. Was I really about to go on a wild goose chase, that could possibly mean getting killed by an age-old legend? *You're damn right I was.*

I unlocked the castle with the original skeleton key and pushed the heavy doors out of my way. Taking in a deep breath and then coughing up all the dust I had just inhaled, since I hadn't cleaned this room yet, I walked through the first foyer and found the staircase again like on the first day. I climbed the massive staircase and when I had finally got to the top landing, I had to hunch over and take a breather. I had forgotten how many stairs there were. I clutched onto the banister, knowing that rushing around was making me short of breath at the moment.

Feeling better, I started for the last room on the right down the left-hand hallway. When I reached the door, something made me rethink why I was there. I was following the writings of what most would call a mad man, making up stories about princes that have been cursed, or evil witches that want revenge. Was I mad for wanting all the pieces to make sense?

After almost having an existential crisis, I turned the door knob to the room with the odd staircase. Letting the cool air of the empty room hit my face, I spotted the stairs. I walked over to the start of the wooden post that would lead me down through the wall and into the basement, but before I did that, I looked around.

I looked closely at the walls of the room and if I squinted hard enough with the flashlight I had had on the whole time, I almost saw molding around the baseboards and ceiling. They were tiny horses running in a line, something a small child would like, something for a nursery. This could have been the prince's nursery before he was cursed. I swung my flashlight onto the staircase below me and started down them, one at a time. I ducked underneath the wall that the stairs went through and descended into the dark basement.

The basement hadn't changed in the couple days since I went down here, but it did feel like a cold wind blew through moments before I had come down the stairs. It was still dark and dank, with no natural light even if the sun had been up. Remembering that it was about three in the morning, I realized that even if I get out of here before school started, I would probably sleep through all of my classes anyways.

I looked at each door as I went by and when I finally reached the end, I stopped. I looked at the great big iron door, with the little wisps of silver running through it. Two things that shouldn't go together and, in all honesty, should have exploded when being melted to make this door. Maybe there was more magic than just the prince at work here. I assumed the rest of the room was made out of the same material, otherwise the prisoner could escape through the wall if he made a hole or something.

I felt for the silver key in my pants pocket and brought it out. The metal was still cool to the touch even with it being in my pocket for nearly an hour. I walked closer to the door and reached out with the key. My hand didn't shake, and I wasn't scared; the energy and vibe surrounding the door should have made me want to run for the hills, but I pressed on.

I hoped this key would work, because I was out of options and the tension would kill me. Not knowing what was really on the other side of that door, I slipped the key into the hole and nearly dropped it when it slid in place. The shock that ran from the iron and silver of the door, ran through the key and into my entire body.

I shook off the zap that made the rest of me go a bit numb, and turned the key to the right, earning a thick click in response. After the click sounded off from the door, a medley of

41

cogs, pulleys and gears seemed to groan in defense; as if they didn't want to be woken up. The key working was all I cared about at the moment, despite the fact that the iron and silver door was now opening for me.

When the door began opening on its own, an unnatural gust of wind came out of nowhere and blew right over me. There was a putrid smell of what could only be described as a rotting corpse taking a bath with a skunk. I had to plug my nose to keep from barfing right there in front of the door.

I shined the flashlight into the room and swung it around a couple of times to see if there was a dead body in there or something. The book's warnings were at the back of my mind, but I ignored them to the best of my abilities. When I looked at the far back wall without going into the room itself, I had to do a double take because I could have sworn, I saw two blood red colored eyes looking back at me.

Before I could try and see what I really saw in the corner of the room, a deep and low voice spoke out to me, locking my body against the wall with fear. "Looks like my knight has finally come."

The unbelievably raspy voice made my heart and body jump, and the eyes that I didn't want to believe I had seen started coming towards me.

Time Lapse

Sitting straight up in bed, tangled in the quilt I was covered in, sweat dripped down my forehead while I looked around the room I was in. Nothing about it looked familiar but nothing felt out of place, it was like I was in a gray area like when you dream. Where was I? I barely remember anything before falling asleep, I definitely didn't remember this bedroom. I looked around the room and noticed that nothing was covered in dust, it was completely clean.

If this was a room at the castle which was the only other place I went to since that week, then this was a room I'd never been in before. I looked at the walls and around the ceiling and noticed the same molding at the stair room. This must have been the prince's old room, but I'd been in his old nursery and it wasn't this clean; what was really going on?

I didn't want to move from my spot for fear that if it wasn't a dream, I would get into serious trouble. Why couldn't I remember anything from before I woke up? I racked my brain to try and figure something out. I knew I finished cleaning the kitchen and then I got on my scooter and drove home. I knew I got ready for bed and then laid there not really able to fall asleep.

Had I sleepwalked all the way to the castle?

I pulled the large quilt off my body and noticed I was wearing a really old looking nightgown. The sleeves were long and ended with very large ruffles that were completely unnecessary. I turned to where my feet dangled off the bed and saw that my feet were perfectly clean, nothing amiss there, if I had sleepwalked then they would be dirty or something, not spotless.

Looking further into what I was wearing and the items around me, I noticed that the bed was also a sight to see. Four

43

posters that were draped with heavy material. It was deep red in color, making it seem more and more royal. The wood of the bed frame was carved with intricate designs and it made me feel like I was stuck in the past, like I had time jumped backwards.

The second I thought those words, the door began to open; not wanting to be seen by anything or anyone stepping into the possible psychotic break I was apparently having, I ran quickly to the large wardrobe that was in the room and jumped into it, closing the doors tight as I waited for the mysteries to unfold.

Before my eyes and through the crack in the door to the wardrobe, I saw a well-dressed man that held himself above the rest, make his way into the room. When he looked back to the door, he watched as a small boy no more than five years old followed behind him. I knew they would see the bed that wasn't made and for some reason, that worried me.

I looked over at the bed and when I did, I had to stifle a gasp because the place I was lying on not minutes before was now made up as if no one had slept in it. What the hell was going on? Was I stuck in some elaborate dream?

Instead of freaking out like I should have been, I decided to watch the scene in front of me and see if that didn't trigger me enough to wake up.

The little boy followed after the old man and right behind him was a lovely lady in a dress that didn't do her justice. She was tall, especially for a woman, and she looked at the little boy with pride in her eyes. She followed behind the small boy that I could only assume was her son and went into the room with him and the other man. "What do you think Cyrus, is this room going to be big enough for you?" The clean and sturdy man asked the excited little boy, who was currently riffling through the blankets on the bed, testing them out. "Why do I have to move to a big boy room, I like my other room, it has all my toys!" The little boy was protesting and when he huffed and puffed, and crossed his arms in further protest, the lovely lady standing by the man walked over to him. "My sweet boy, we need that room for someone very special, and this room can only be lived in by a special prince. Now, if you do not want it then maybe we could find an even more special prince to fill in for you." She used an age-old mother trick to get her son to agree with something they wanted and with the redness of his cheeks and the pout on his lip, she knew she had him. "Wait mummy, I want the room. Because there isn't anyone more special than me, and I am a prince. Who will take the other room?" He dropped his pouty lip and looked at his mother who had a twinkle in her eye and a smile on her lips. So far so good, dream wise. "Well your father and I want you to know that you are going to be a big brother. And your new brother or sister is going sleep in that room, while you take care of this one." She brushed his hair down with the hand and just from where I was standing, in the wardrobe, I could feel the love she had for her son. "I am going to be a brother? That is brilliant, mummy!" The little boy started jumping up and down in front of his parents' smiling faces. Before I could take another breath, the room began to change and the wardrobe I was in was no longer around me. Colors swirled around me making me close my eyes and when I opened them, I found myself standing in the middle of a small room with, who I know now to be the king and the little prince, pacing in front of a door. "Mummy is going to be fine, right?" The prince spoke to his father. I stood there not knowing where to hide when I realized they couldn't see me anyways. I guessed *vivid dream* was now on the table of *what the hell is going on*. "She will be fine son, do not fret." When the king finished talking, a door swung open and a maid rushed over to him. Whispering something to the king, he dashed off through the door. Before the prince could get to it, the door had already closed, and he was too small to reach the knob.

I watched as the prince paced as his father once had before the king had made another appearance. When the king came through the door, again a scream and wail could be heard behind the door. I wasn't sure if I could physically do anything in this dream but staying where I was seemed safer. The king bent down to the prince's level so that he could tell him what was going on. "Son! This isn't easy for me to tell you, but your new baby sister did not make it. She passed away soon after her eyes opened son, and your mother is taking it hard, so it would be best to stay out here." The prince nodded his head, but it didn't seem like he was okay with the news at all. The king stood up and made his way out of the room, away from his wife.

I walked in front of the little prince and bent down to his level, knowing he couldn't see me, I looked at him straight in the eyes and saw his tears running down his face. When his eyes made contact with mine the room changed again, only this time I was left staring at the opened door to the prison cell in the basement of the castle.

I pinched my arm and felt the slight sting of it, in all honesty I don't think that really told me if I was awake or not. But what did were the two red eyes staring back at me, and in a rush of information I got flashes of what happened before the vivid dream hit my head all at once, like the last few hours slapped me in the face.

I don't know how to say it or describe it, but something in that room made me go back in time to see the prince's mother lose a child, and I didn't know what it meant. Before I could move away from the stone wall I was leaning against, a voice rang through the room in front of me. "You really are a knight, only a knight of the Black lineage could open that door. Tell me knight, are you here to kill me, or set me free?"

His raspy voice gained confidence and volume, but I didn't know what to tell the figure, because I wasn't a knight even if I came from the Black line and I had a feeling if he knew that, he would be incredibly pissed off. Because if this was the prince the dream was talking about, and the book, and the children's story, then he thought I was the curse breaker and I didn't know how to tell him that I was just the person who inherited his castle and that I didn't want anything to do with him or this curse, but I needed to try something. "I'm not a knight, I'm just here to see the castle that was passed on to me recently. I was told by a man in a fancy hat that this castle belongs to me now." My voice wasn't as strong as it should have been, and I knew that; I just hoped he didn't notice.

I took in a shaky breath and looked back to where the red eyes had been, but in a flash of cold air and blurred shadows, a figure had me pinned against the wall behind me. The stone wall bit into my back and with my eyes now shut I held my breath, not only because it smelled but because I was worried breathing might piss him off. "Open your eyes, not knight." I almost wanted to laugh at this thing's passive aggressive attitude, but of course I didn't.

I opened my eyes and the man before me, if you could even call him that, was pale and his skin looked like it would fall off at any moment. The little boy in the dream was cute and adorable and he grew into this... this thing; the curse had made his skin scaly and in sections of it seemed like he had peeled pieces of it off. His iris was blood red but luckily the whites of his eyes were normal, just a bit yellow from age, his lips were cracked and bleeding and the teeth that showed were nothing but yellow and sharp like the point of a knife.

His face didn't scare me, his stench didn't completely repulse me, and his eyes had no other effect on me. But this thing in front of me was definitely the little prince from the dream. Only he grew up and got into some trouble; from what I'd read anyways. "Cyrus." It wasn't a question and he wasn't going to answer it. I just needed him to know I knew who he was.

He closed his eyes for a second and then opened them to reveal their not so red shade anymore, no, his eyes were completely and utterly black, the whites and all.

Leather Bound Lies

His breathing was harsh and vile, something like a zombie's breath might smell like. But this was no zombie, well not in the traditional sense. His black eyes met mine and as I looked closer into them, I could see that the black came from the veins that now visibly surrounded underneath his eyes. The more I looked at the veins, the more it looked like poison running underneath his skin.

I know I should be scared and worried that at any moment he could kill me and be set free on the town below him, but I knew one thing; he needed me. Even if I wasn't a knight, he thought I was and I knew that would make me valuable for a while. I just needed to get him talking and get that black out of his eyes, because the red was bad but the black was so much worse. "I read about you, that's how I found you down here. I read a book and it felt familiar, so I thought back to a story I was told before bed about a knight protecting a prince. I connected the dots and the random situation of me coming into ownership of the castle on the hill when I have no family members that have ever lived here to my knowledge, except for the first knight they brought here. It's all connected… so please don't kill me, I could be of use." I rambled on and on and hoped that he was dull enough to accept my pleas for life. "The books are all lies." He stepped back after those five words and walked back into the cell, I had just freed him from. I cocked my head to the side and wondered what he was doing back in that very smelly room.

He disappeared into the darkness of the cell and when I flashed my light in there, he started coming back out with something in his hand. He walked towards me and this time, I didn't tense up and cower against the wall behind me. He brought up the item he had brought from the room, handed it to

48

me with a push and then turned away from me, heading towards the staircase.

I looked down at the very large and heavy object in my hands and when I turned it over I realized it was a book; a really old and smelly book. It didn't have the same smell as a normal book would, it didn't smell like paper and leather. Instead, it smelled like the room in front of me and when I opened the cover, I had to stop my eyes from falling out of my head because it looked just like his skin did, falling apart at the seams.

Hurrying behind the prince and up the stairs, I realized he probably hadn't been out of that room since his father locked him in there. That was back in the 1600s, maybe early 1700s. As I caught up to him and kept looking at the book I felt the thick, oddly shaped pages of something other than paper. The ink that was used was definitely not ink and it was bound with something that again wasn't normal for a book. "Where did you get this book? It's odd." I trailed behind him as he sniffed around his old home, seeing it for the first time in over three hundred years. "I wrote it. That is the real story, not some leather bound lie you have been reading. Tell me that you have been keeping up with this place since you are the new owner." He stopped in the hall outside his old nursery where the stairs that lead to his capture had been. He turned and headed for the kitchen like I was. "I was told a few days ago about the new property I now own, I followed the book trail instead of cleaning, so it isn't as clean as it should be by now." I shrugged my shoulders and stood by the kitchen island and watched him look around some more.

He looked back with an almost amused look on his cracked face. The more I looked at his face, the more I saw what the curse had really done to him. It completely turned him into a monster, by looks alone so far. I hadn't really seen what he was like, personality wise anyways. "If you wrote it, how did you get the materials for it? Being trapped in that room for over three hundred years I don't suppose you magically grew a tree to make paper." My snide comment didn't go unnoticed and when he stopped mid-walk, I had to as well. I looked up at him and his very slender figure and waited for a response. He was so skinny, practically bone and skin and of course the overly grown hair on his head. "Three hundred years? So what year is it now?" A look of worry flashed on his face, but he covered it up rather quickly. I didn't figure he stopped keeping up with the date while being a prisoner. "It's 2014, when were you first imprisoned?" I knew some details from the book, but I wanted to hear it from him. His look of complete loss wasn't lost on me. I took a seat on a stool and put the weird book in my lap. He walked around, looking at everything that was now uncovered from the dust. "My birth year is 1690 and I was cursed and thrown away by my father in the year 1707, so that was about three hundred and seven years ago. I did not think that much time had passed. Tell me something fake knight, where are you really from? You do not sound of England." He looked right at me and when his eyes flashed from the red to the black and back again, I knew he wasn't going to let me not tell him. I rolled my eyes and started my side of the story. "My sister and I moved here from America because she had a job offer that she couldn't refuse, and we needed to leave our other lives behind. That's it, so are you going to tell me how you made this book?" I put the book on the counter in front of me and started flipping the thick pages around. "I will say this, those are not made of paper, the ink is not ink and the string used to bind it is not string. Keep in mind I had no way of getting paper, or ink, or string while I was in there." I listened to what he said and thought about what he would have used, and when I came to an idea, I quickly stopped touching the book. "You used blood for the ink, you peeled pieces of flesh that was already coming off of your body for the pages which is why they are so jagged and thick and why they are stitched together since you couldn't get a big enough piece for a whole page, and then you used your hair for the binding; didn't you?" I was creeped out to say the least and the way he looked over the book in sheer pride made me want to barf. I guess, I watched too many serial killer documentaries. "You would have done the same thing if every second of your imprisonment was filled with pain, anguish, a hunger that will never die, and a never-ending loop of your worst memories playing in your head. Now, tell me that I am the one that is insane. You should be giving that look to my father." His bitterness and spite was seeping out of every word he spoke.

Being trapped somewhere for three hundred and seven years sounded like torture, but to be under that much pain and put through every wrong thing you had ever done in your life, that was the real torture.

He walked closer to where I was sitting on the stool. His face came closer and closer to mine and I suddenly felt all the sleep that I had been missing at one time. His eyes were curious and the gross book that now sat on the counter was weighing in my mind. I wondered what it said, what he wrote in it and why. If there were stories that he said were wrong out there, like the one I was reading, then what was the real story?

I took this chance to look at his face at a better angle. His skin was peeling off his face, the skin that was still on there was so pale and the dark sacks under his eyes were predominant against his high cheekbones and sunken face. He looked utterly sick. He closed his eyes and took in a deep breath. Letting out his breath, his red eyes met mine and while I stared at them, I watched the black flow into them from the veins under his skin, if I didn't know any better I would think he was hungry. "Tell me fake knight, are you scared of monsters?" His question posed a thought in my head. Was I scared of real life monsters? No! I didn't think I was, I'd met other monsters in my time and he seemed docile compared to them. "I'm not scared of you, I've read enough to know that you deserved this curse and it seems that you still haven't learned your lesson." It was a very bold move to say something like that in front of someone that could kill me in a swift flick of their wrist. But it was true, I wasn't scared of him. "Then you will not be scared of what I am about to do." Before I had the chance to ask him what he was talking about, he had me by the throat and was pulling me off the stool.

My legs dangled just above the clean floor while his hand tightened around my throat more and more. When I got a good look at him, I watched his face twist and turn into the monster he was cursed to be. His mouth opened, and his canines elongated on the top and bottom, creating four long sharp fangs, his eyes began to bleed the black vein liquid down his face like he was crying. I watched as his jaw unhinged and grew wider and wider. My fear level rose some but at the same time, I still wasn't scared of him, I knew he wouldn't kill me, he could harm me but not kill.

Before my next thought was processed, in a flash he had removed his hand from my neck and held me by the shoulders, making room for him to violently snap his mouth on my throat and begin to tear into my flesh effectively, drinking my blood like a vampire.

The only thoughts going through my head were fuzzy and I kept thinking that he wouldn't kill me; would he?

A Taste for Humanity

Having my life force being forcefully taken from me wasn't as painful as I thought it would be. That could be the fact that it felt like half of my blood supply was being depleted and I was about to pass out or die, I wasn't really paying attention, I was trying to stay awake.

When I barely felt the slight loosening of his grip, I tried to come to enough consciousness to break free of his ironclad grasp. I waited for my moment and when I felt him shift slightly on my shoulders, I took my chance. Raising my arms as swiftly as I could, I was able to knock his hold on me away. I didn't really think it all the way through since I forgot I was dangling about two feet off the ground.

I fell to the kitchen floor, which now had puddles of my blood on it. I clutched my left hip in pain when I realized I smacked it on the stool when I fell down to the ground. I wobbled on my butt until I found a good center of balance and without slipping around in my own blood, I got off the floor and started to make a wobbly path towards the front door of the castle; I needed to get home. Now.

My mind was still fuzzy, and I was going in and out of consciousness, I was surprised I hadn't barfed with all the wobbling my body was doing. Should I dare look back to see if he's following me? Or should I just take my chances and keep wobbling for my life. Seriously, it was like trying to walk on two legs that had fallen asleep.

I wasn't completely sure how much blood he drank but it was enough for me to want to sleep for a few days. I hadn't had this amount of dizziness, cold limbs, and wobbling legs in at least five years, but that story is best saved for later.

I think I had made it to the front door because the blurry thing in front of me looked kind of like the door to the castle. I reached up to my neck and felt the warm blood still flowing out of my throat; I needed something to press against it. At that moment, the only thing I could think of was my shirt I was wearing.

As soon as I stopped to peel off my shirt, a loud and vibrating scream was voiced through the castle. He had obviously been in some sort of trance from the blood to have just now noticed I was gone. Having not had anything to drink, whether it was blood or water for that long, I wasn't surprised he got a little drunk off of it.

I finally got my shirt off my body and was now pressing it against my neck, pushing harder despite the protest of the nerves surrounding the wound. I flinched at the stinging pain of the pressure but pushed through it; I needed to get home. He could deal with himself until I healed.

The screaming had stopped, and I was relieved when I made it to the front door. It felt like the walk to it took a week. I used as much strength as I could give to get the door knob to turn; most of the strength I had left was going into walking and staying awake.

The knob turned, and the heavy door opened with a little help from the wind outside. I could hear his footsteps coming towards the door as I hurried to close it. I knew he couldn't leave the castle that was part of the curse, at least that was a part I really wanted to be true.

Letting the door close tight, I barely missed him slamming his fists into the other side of the door. I held my hand against the door as if to keep it from opening with him banging his fists on the other side. The pressure I kept on the shirt was beginning to stop the bleeding, but for how long I didn't know. I needed him to know that I wasn't abandoning him, that I would be back despite what he did to me. Because even if he thought he could scare me away, this was still my castle and I needed to make a decision, which is why I wasn't too broken up about leaving him now. "I'll come back Cyrus, you need to dry out, and you can't leave this place anyways. So, sit tight and I'll be back another day." I spoke through the pain of the injury on my throat even if it did come out gargled and barely audible. I meant every word I said, I would be back. Part of it was to figure out what I was going to do with the castle and so I could beat his ass for doing this to me, the other part of me wanted to know more about how I was tied to this whole thing, not just my bloodline because there was something else. My sister had always said that my curiosity would get me in trouble one day, I hated it when she's right.

Wobbling over to my scooter and starting it up, I sort of tied the rest of my shirt to my neck and got all the way on the scooter. The sun would be up soon, and I wasn't wearing a top. I needed to get into my house and fast. Hoping I wouldn't pass out while driving home, I made sure I went extra fast, despite the urge to want to barf everywhere, and the road blurring into many different paths.

Somehow, I had driven all the way down the hill and to my front yard without falling off the scooter or passing out in the middle of the road. I was fuzzy about the details of the trip but all I cared about was being home.

I got to the front door and fumbled with my keys. I leaned against the door for more support, my legs had turned into jelly and that wasn't good for walking with. I found the right one and put the key in the hole, turning it I unlocked the door and stumbled into the living room. I didn't bother locking my scooter up because I wouldn't have been able to anyways. Dragging my feet into the kitchen, where I knew we had some antibacterial spray and bandages for my neck wound.

I fumbled around the counters leaving bloody hand prints in my path. Finding the cabinet that had what I needed in it, I grabbed what I could see and tossed it on the floor. Leaning against the counter top and slowing making my way down to the floor to rest and bandage myself up without hurting myself more in the process.

My butt made contact with the cold floor underneath me. I felt around for the spray and the gauze for the bandage. Finding the spray, I removed my shirt and prepared myself for the sting of the medicine. With a shaking hand I pressed the button for the spray and when it made contact with the opened wound I gasped and hissed at the pain it caused.

Throwing down the can of spray, I grabbed the gauze and medical tape from the floor next to my leg. I put a good amount of gauze on the wound and the coiled the rest around my neck for support. Taking the medical tape, I taped the sides of the gauze down so that stuff wouldn't get into it while it healed. Throwing all the supplies down and putting my shaking hands into my lap, I took in a needed breath.

My back ached against the hard cabinets and my butt was going numb while sitting on the tiled floor. I peeked around the kitchen and saw patches of my blood in various places. I needed to clean the kitchen, and probably the living room. I needed a shower too, but first maybe a little nap. My eyelids began to slowly close while the scene around me began to blur out of focus; just a little nap.

Nagging Little Voice

Waking up from a blood loss induced nap was like trying to clear away a frosted window without a heater in the middle of December. There was this far off bell sound that kept dinging away in my head and I wasn't sure if it was actually coming from my head, or if something else was making the sound, but it forced me to clear away the frost even faster. The more and more I sat there and listened, the more it sounded like a doorbell.

Oh crap! The doorbell!

Someone was at the door and here I was trying to come out of a blood loss induced sleep with blood still all over the counters, no shirt and a large bandage on my neck; great, just great.

I finally focused on everything in the room long enough to stand up from the floor. Getting my balance back, I walked to the living room where the ding donging just got louder. I looked for anything to cover myself up with and settled on the blanket on the back of the couch. I wrapped myself up in the blanket and walked to the door. If it was the guy in the suit again, I was going to punch him in the face. This was his fault, he started this and I was sticking with that story for now.

Not having a peep hole on the door, I had to just open it and find out who was on the other side. I swung the door open and when the sun hit my eyes, it was like being slapped in the face. I closed my eyes within a second of meeting the sun's glare and didn't even get a look at who was actually ringing my doorbell. "Oh! I didn't know you were sick, why are you walking around if you're sick?" Margaret's voice cut through the sun's rays and made it to my ears. I had forgotten that I was going to come by her store yesterday, things got a bit crazy. "Sorry, I'm not sick; please come in, the sun is being a menace." I stepped aside to let her by and when I turned back to the living room, I opened my eyes and let them adjust back to the dim light of the living room. "If you aren't sick, why aren't you in school? Don't tell me you've been drinking!" Margaret played the doting aunt card like she had always done for my sister and me. "No! Why would you think I've been drinking?" She took a seat on the couch and I sat at the other end of it. Making sure she didn't see me up close and personal. "You have bags under your eyes, you're wearing a blanket when it's the middle of spring, you seem hung over, and you skipped school for no reason. And what happened to your neck?" The last worry was a lot more surprised than I thought she would ever be towards me. I mean, she saw my sister and me the day that we moved here. That day I was covered head to toe in bruises practically, just as pale and avoiding eye contact as well. Maybe she didn't connect the dots. "Well! I'm not hungover, I just had a rough night last night and most of this morning. What day is it? Isn't it Wednesday?" I asked her and watched the worry increase on her face. "Yeah, it's Wednesday. It's Wednesday afternoon. It's like 3 p.m., that's why I thought you would be in school. I wanted to come by and talk to Olivia." She looked around where we were sitting as if to find her, her English accent always made me smile, especially when she said Olivia's name. I had always wished that I took on the English accent after moving here but I was stuck with my plain old American one.

"I've just been a bit worn out because of the work I've been doing on the old castle. It came into my name randomly; they said they had been tracking me down for years but whatever. I accidently got jabbed by something on the wall there and it broke the skin, not a big deal." I waved her off and kept my voice even so that she didn't think I was lying about anything.

I wanted to tell her the truth, that the book she gave me wasn't a myth and that the prince was still alive. But knowing all of this had put my life in more danger than before and I wasn't going to risk her life being in danger too. But on the other hand, how would the prince know?

She may be someone who gets lost in books like I do but there is a difference between reading, collecting, and loving them then there is in actually living them, and she didn't seem like the person that would want to leave her safe zone for a story. "Well, I came to tell Olivia that I received a call about a couple named Maurice and Monica Shepard, something about their court date for their new placement is being moved up and they needed to tell their next of kin, and that there is a possibility that they could be released due to good behavior or something. To tell you the truth I wasn't listening." She told me the news with the wave of her hand, not knowing that those two names were the ones we ran from. "The court date has been changed?" I looked down at my hand and tried to stop the angry tears from forming in my eyes. I knew they would get out of system somehow, I knew a life sentence was too good to be true. They had to have bribed the right people; no person in their right minds would let them loose on this world. "Yeah, are they family members of yours?" I looked up at her and gave her a fake smile that I hoped she bought. "Yeah, distant aunt and uncle, got into a bit of trouble when they were younger, and it came back to bite them in the butt. I guess we are the only family they have left. Weird. Why did you get the call?" I questioned her and hoped she wouldn't question my story. "Well, since the Mayor is out of town, he sanctioned my store to be the one that gets all the calls for the town for the next month. It's really annoying but I thought I would give the message in person. Why wouldn't they call your parents?" That word nearly made me flinch.

Parents, that's not what I would call them.

I tried to think of something else, like Cyrus locked up in that castle again and when I pictured him banging on the front doors, I thought I could almost hear his voice calling out for me to come back. It was like a small nagging voice at the back of my mind. I easily brushed off the idea and looked back at Margaret. "I guess you caught me there. Maurice and Monica aren't my aunt and uncle, they are our *parents,* but we don't talk about them because they are very bad people. When we ran away from them five years ago, they had been told that they would serve two life sentences each, but I guess that wasn't true. We didn't check up on their cases because we don't want anything to do with them."

"Is that why you two have different last names? How bad could they have been to receive life in prison, twice? Well, I guess they didn't, but still." She shrugged her shoulders and I had to tell myself that they were still a country away; they couldn't hurt me at this moment in time. I needed to get ready for them though, they weren't going to try and take my life away again. "Their last names are the last names and their first names, they used when they went on the run after we were born; we switched back to our mother's maiden name, that's what's on our birth certificate. They've had several different names and were bad even before we were born. My sister got us out of there as soon as she was old enough. We don't talk about it because those two are monsters. And honestly, the fact that they conned themselves new hearings doesn't surprise me, it isn't the first time it's happened." I let my tears fall and didn't hold anything back; I needed this out in the open. "They will come for us if they get out of prison; we were the ones that turned them in. We were asked to stay out of the papers and everyone was told that they didn't have kids. That's what kept us safe, that and moving to a new country." I wiped my face on the blanket wrapped around me and stared at the fabric in my hands. "Sweetheart, what did they do?" I really didn't want to tell her this part, but it was something that couldn't stay bottled up anymore, the nightmares alone had been driving me insane. "They killed a lot of people." I looked her in the eye and waited for my moment to bare it all to her.

The Story of My Life

Breathe, breathe... Stop shaking, it's just a talk. It's just a talk.

Having to remind myself to breathe and stay calm wasn't a good sign, but when did I even listen to the signs. My sister had always told me that no one would understand why our parents were the way they are, people would be scared of us and no one would want to be around us if they knew the truth. Plus, it was dangerous; it would put our lives in danger again and it would put the person listening to the story in danger. But this was Margaret. Sweet book shop owner Margaret, who can hold her head high and talk sweetly to me, while fending off anyone that tries to do harm in her store. She of all people might understand.

I watched her wait for me to go on but she sensed my hesitation. Instead, I watched her stand up, walk through the doors to the kitchen and when she started screaming, I remembered I hadn't cleaned up the blood on the counters. I flinched at her scream and decided that I might have to tell her the truth about that as well. If not, she was going to think the worst and I was just getting to know her.

Taking in another deep breath and hearing her open and close the refrigerator without another peep; she walked back through the kitchen door and sat back on the couch. Handing me a piece of cheese and a bottle of water, she looked at me to continue. I ate the cheese in one bite, not realizing it had been over a day since I last eaten anything. The look on her face as she glanced back to the revolving door of the kitchen probably wondering what really happened in there. I watched her eyes trail back up to the bandage on my neck and then she looked away without another word.

I took a swig of the water and sat the bottle on the coffee table then let out a shaky breath. "You have to understand that this conversation is going to be hard for me, but my sister and I trust you and I think it's time you knew why we moved to this country." I eyed her expression after I spoke and looked for a reason to continue. When I saw her look at me, I gathered the confidence I needed to keep going. "My parents met in the nineties when they were in their late teens. My father came from a sadistic household that only shaped the way his outlook on life was. His father was a known rapist and abuser, my father grew up around that and came to know that as his only way of life. When he met my mother, she only encouraged him to expand his horizons when it came to his extracurricular activities."

I ignored the fear hiding in the back of my mind and kept going. "My mother's back story is unknown to me or my sister, all I know is she is just as bad as he is." My words broke as I spoke about the people that put us through a literal hell. "After my sister was born they had gone underground, they were close to being caught for killing several college students around the state they were living in, college students were their favorite. When my sister was born, they changed their names for the hundredth time and our mother gave Olivia her maiden name; they also adopted a suburban lifestyle for a while. Even with my sister being a toddler, it didn't stop them from doing their extracurricular activities." I glared at a spot on the wall at the memory of reading all about them like they were strangers in the newspaper. "My sister was four years old when my mother found out she was pregnant again. They despised us, and we knew it from a young age. They were barely around us when we were small and as we got to school age, they kept us out of it whenever they were about to get caught. They feared that we would tell a teacher about what went on in that house, even though my father swore we didn't know anything, but our mom was paranoid. When I was born, my sister was a few months away from being six and even at her young age she took care of me as much as a five-year-old could." I held back the tears that wanted to fall because if I started crying then I wouldn't finish the story. "After I was old enough to walk, they never stayed in one place for longer than a month. They went from state to state killing teenagers and running away. My sister would keep me away from them whenever possible. They had never laid a hand on us, not at that age. I heard stories and promises every night from Olivia, saying she would take us away from here after she turned eighteen, because otherwise they could tell social services that we were runaways. They always feared that we would leave them and tell everyone, I always asked Olivia why they didn't just give us up as soon as we were born but she didn't know the answer."

Remembering the cold nights when we squatted in an abandoned house before our parents made their next move hurt me. I could feel the cold from the memory and it was like I was back in those abandoned houses. The cold grew on my skin as it did then, I wanted to shiver from the memory but when I realized I wasn't actually in that house, the cold went away, and I clutched the blanket tighter to me. Seeing the pain my sister was still in, made me clutch the blanket's edge tighter. Remembering that she flinched at every outside noise because it reminded her of our parents coming after her. Thinking about all the night terrors she had and when she would wake me up in the middle of the night. Knowing that she will be messed up for the rest of her life, probably never being able to have a healthy relationship with anyone but me. I knew I would have to take care of her in a different way than she took care of me, and it will be forever.

Just thinking about my sister in general and how she will forever be messed up because of these people made me nearly rip the blanket I had in my hands. I hated that I turned out partially normal and she got the raw end of the deal; she had to live with all the crushing anxiety, and the fear that I could be taken away from her at any point. There were times that our parents even threatened to kill me just to get her to do things because they knew she would do whatever they wanted just to keep me safe; but at what cost? "Now when my sister turned into a teenager she became less and less happy, and she didn't seem like herself anymore. I later found out it was because my father had started abusing her and when my mother found out, she became jealous that she was taking her husband away. It was sick, they were sick. The day my sister turned eighteen, she took all the saving she had from doing side work for a local robotics organization and moved us out here. She told me at the time that it was because she had a job offer and that wasn't a complete lie. She was brilliant from day one and it showed in her work. She was never the same after we left, I thought maybe being away from them would make the smile come back to her face, but she just stayed to herself."

I talked about my sister, my guardian angel, like she was dead. But I knew that when Friday rolled around, she would be home, and our lives would go back to the normalcy she had built for the both of us. If only that was the truth, because with Cyrus in the picture I wasn't sure what was going to happen. I knew if I told Olivia the truth she would just put it to the back of her mind and lock it away for safe keeping like she did with everything else. That's why if you asked her about our parents, she would just say they were dead or away, she denied everything after we left, it was like she tried to bleach them from her memory. "I knew you two were running from something when you came into town, but I had no idea." Her soft words were comforting to me, but she still couldn't understand the whole picture. "If they get out, they won't stop until they find us. We were the ones that called the cops before we boarded that plane. We told them where to find our parents and we were granted a private life and the news teams were told they didn't have children. I think that's how they knew it was us. We were protected from the news but not from them. Even if they were killers, they were still off the charts smart. That's where Olivia gets it from, our parents, they were really smart." I remembered seeing their plans on the kitchen table one night when I woke up, and I remember the screaming and harsh words that told me to go back to sleep. But what I saw was complicated and confusing, plus they never got caught until we called them in.

My skin crawled with the words that had left my lips, I didn't know what we would do if they get out and found us. The one thing they were good at, besides raping and killing women, was tracking things down. They would find us and the only thing we could do was run, but Cyrus was at the back of my mind telling me to stay. "You know I'm not only answering phones for the Mayor, I'm acting on his behalf. So, I can put up a sign in every business and main building in this town telling people not to let them in. I can even put some at our borders to try and stop them. If that will make you feel safer, I'll do it."

She reached her hand and placed it on my knee. I felt the warmth from her wanting us to be safe flow through her hand and into me. It was nice to meet an adult that wanted to help us. "I think that would be good." I gave her a slight smile and looked back down at my hands that I covered in the blanket. "You know the book you traded me for?" She sat back up and nodded yes. "It's not just a legend or story, Margaret. It's real, and I found him." I smiled for the first time for real that night. And as I watched her eyes go from me to the couch and then back to me, I thought she might think I was crazy or that I also bumped my head when I got this neck wound. "You mean he's still alive?" Her question threw me off guard. "You knew that he was real the whole time?" *She couldn't have, right?* "My family tree goes way back to when his family was still in power, before the monarchy died out. I wrote the first book about his curse, I wrote the book I gave you under a different name. I was there the day everything fell apart. When his mother, our queen died and everything. I can't believe he's still alive, I guess the rumors then are still true now." The words she spoke weren't processing properly in my head, because it sounded like she said she was alive when he was still human. "Are you telling me you're over three hundred years old?" I asked her, wanting like hell to know the truth. "I am. How do you think I have all of those books? And to be specific, I'm four hundred and six years old. But in my species years, I'm around forty, that's why I look around forty to everyone else." She nonchalantly spoke about being four centuries old like it wasn't a big deal. "What species would that be?" I held my breath and hoped she didn't say something like ghoul or something. "A witch; I don't go bragging about it since the Salem witch trial bullshit, but you're getting closer to our world and I figured it wouldn't hurt to tell you." My mouth hung open in shock and awe, she was a witch; yeah, this day was turning out to be just as weird as the day before.

Ask and You Shan't Receive

My chest felt heavy as I tried to breathe through the pain of another slice to my skin. I felt the tense arm of my mother holding me down on the table as she kept slicing into my most important arteries. I squirmed and wiggled trying to get out of her grasp, but it only made her press harder.

I wanted to scream for my sister, for anyone that was willing and able to hear my voice, but the gag in my mouth was barely letting air into my lungs, let alone letting anything out of it.

My head was pounding and the sweat from the pain and torture I was going through was getting into my eyes and burning the corners of my lids as it dripped down the side of my face. I knew I was crying but the sounds of my gagged screams were more important than the sound of my crying. My vision was blurry as I looked up at the woman that called herself my mother. I wanted so badly for my sister to save me but I didn't know where she was and every second that passed by was another slice to my legs, or my arms, even my throat.

I was bleeding out slowly and losing consciousness along with it. I needed to stay awake because if my sister got here, she wouldn't be able to lift me up completely by herself. She was only seventeen for a few more hours and I think my parents knew we were going to leave them. I could feel the anger rolling off of her after every hit, every new slice of my flesh. She was going to kill me like all the other girls they have killed. I needed to get out. I needed out. I needed out!

'Wake up. Wake up. Wake up.'

Jolting awake from what I can only assume was one of the worst nightmares I had ever had, with the lingering voice in my head telling me to wake up, I looked around the room I was in and tried to remember the last few hours before I got in here. It almost felt like someone was in the room with me trying to wake me up.

I remembered telling that story to Margaret and then telling her about the prince, but I didn't remember her leaving and me going to sleep. I looked over at the clock on my nightstand and saw that it was two in the morning. Can't I ever sleep completely through the night?

I groaned and dragged my legs and the rest of my sweaty body out of my bed and to the bathroom for a much-needed shower.

I gingerly peeled off the bandage from my neck and saw the mangled flesh underneath. I shivered when I saw the teeth marks and the pieces that wanted to just fall right off. I should have gotten stitches, but people would ask too many questions. Leaving the bandage off and being extremely careful, I took off the bottoms I was wearing and my bra, I jumped into the shower and started the warm water.

Letting the heat warm my bones and being careful not let the wound too far into the heavy stream of water, I carefully began to bathe myself.

Stepping over the tub's side and getting out of the shower, I reached for a towel to wrap myself into in an attempt to get away from the shivering cold of the room.

I made sure my hair didn't get in my neck wound before I bandaged it again and then got dressed. I put some more spray on it and new gauze, making sure the medical tape was secure. I started drying off the rest of my body. I ran the towel over my front and my back and trailed it down and over my wet legs. I stopped when a flash from the nightmare before triggered after I passed over my inner thigh.

The sensation of my mother running the scalpel over my femoral artery and cutting the skin above it, creating a pool of blood that fell over my leg and onto the table she had me strapped to.

I shook the image out of my head and looked down at my leg, there was no line of blood dripping down it, there was no table underneath me, and I was fine. Safe.

I finished toweling off and getting dressed, trying not to remember any sort of image from before. I needed to clear my head and what better way than going back to the castle and cleaning up like I wanted to do, so I could figure out what I was going to do with the freaking castle I now owned and the creepy crawly man child playing host in it. School wouldn't miss me for a couple more days.

I had everything that I needed in my bag which included snacks this time. The weird thing was that when I went into the kitchen, there was no trail of blood on the counters anymore. Margaret must have cleaned it up. I knew it was nearly three in the morning and no one in their right mind was awake, which I was thankful for. No need for the extra questions my sneaking around in the middle of the night would bring.

I started my scooter and secured my bag before I let go of the ground and the brake, allowing the scooter to do its intended job. The scooter lurched into action and carried me down the road. When I looked forward at the castle, my destination, I wondered whose shadow my eyes thought they saw that day? Was It Cyrus? It couldn't have been if he was locked away in the basement. Maybe there is more to his story that I still haven't heard.

I still didn't understand the paperwork either. They thought I was from a line of knights, but I was barely a functioning teenager. Why did that man pick me? I'm not a knight, or a long-lost princess, or even from this damn country, so why show up at my door step? Why not sell the place after all these years of not being able to find the next person in line and being turned down by my mother and her father before that? Why go to all the trouble?

My thoughts made me lose focus on the road for one second and when I did, my scooter seemed to have a mind of its own because it ran into something. And when I looked up, I realized it was someone.

I picked myself and the scooter off the ground looking for any sign of the person I ran over at three in the morning. When I landed on a crumpled-up man that was now staggering to his feet, I felt relief that I didn't hurt him. "Gregory is that you?" I wanted to slap myself for running into him and his big head. Knowing him, he would hold it over my head until he died.

He looked at me with a weird gaze, like he hadn't seen me in years which was odd because I had seen him last Tuesday. The closer I looked at him, the more it seemed like he was drunk off his ass then curious as to why I was sitting on my scooter in front of him. "Henrietta? Is that you?" His accent came out in a slur of mispronounced words. I was surprised he got my name right. I shook my head and parked the scooter for a second. I got off and took him by the arm, leading him to the sidewalk and out the way of everyone else, I made sure he was okay before I left.

Getting back on my scooter and starting it up again, I looked over to see him still staring at me. "The teachers said you were sick or something, but you don't look sick." His voice was louder than it should have been, and his words were long and slurred. It wasn't surprising that he drunk on a school night, at least I didn't hurt him when he was in the middle of the road. I was actually glad he was drunk because he wouldn't remember this in the morning. "Go home and drink some water, Gregory. I'm fine." I clicked my helmet into place and took off without another word. I needed to find out why I was the one picked that day. And I had a feeling Cyrus and his book knew more than they said.

The drive to the castle wasn't long and the more crap I took up there, the less time it seemed to take. I parked my scooter and wasted no time in unlocking the intimidating door and going inside. The dust was flying around my head and face like glitter as if someone had just walked through here. I kept going through the castle, until I landed on the kitchen again.

Before I looked around it, my eyes landed on the book Cyrus had so crudely made out of himself. I didn't want to touch it again, but I needed to know what it said. "Are you done throwing your fit and decided to rejoin the party?" Cyrus' voice came out of nowhere and from behind me and into my ears. I paid him no mind, he knew what he did was wrong, and I wasn't giving him the satisfaction of having me cower in his presence. I didn't cower to anyone anymore. "I don't know, are you done being a brat?" I rebutted. "Hmm, you know when the witch killed me that night, she said the only way for the curse to be broken is to find someone that can love me in spite of what I have done and love the beast I have become. When they sent you here, I did not think you would be so unwilling to work with me." He circled forward and in front of the kitchen island keeping his red eyes on my still not responding body. "How did you make a shadow appear in the window that day if you haven't been out of the room in three hundred years? How did that man find me when I'm not technically a *Black* that I know of, and therefore not of the line of knights you need? And how did you know someone was going to send me to you when you've said you have had no contact with anyone?" My questions came out of my mouth faster than I thought they would and some of them didn't make sense once they left my head and came into the surrounding air. "So many questions for such a small girl." His yellow teeth showed as his lips parted in a crooked smile. "The size of my body does not dwindle the importance of my questions. Answer them or be locked back in that room for the rest of eternity. Because I'll make sure no one else even looks at this castle." I was done with his games, all he wanted was the blood in my veins and a way out of his curse, his deserving curse.

Five Years of Waiting

I should have been thumbing through the disgusting book right now, but I wasn't. Instead, I was having a staring match with a three-hundred-year-old toddler. I had to keep telling myself I wouldn't break before he did but on the other hand he didn't need to blink, he could have his eyes open for a year and be fine, I was sure. I took the high road and blinked my eyes, turning my face away from him, I started with the book again. "Why do you want answers to all those questions anyways? Why can you not just come along for the ride and be ignorant?" I scoffed at him, did he really think I was that sort of person, someone that could just be used and thrown away, I had been that way with my parents and I wasn't going to be that way ever again. "Of course, you want me to be ignorant, that way you can get what you want out of this situation while I do the hard part. Then, you'll have your life back and I will be nothing more than a plain teenager living out her life until she dies a plain death. But here's where you get it wrong, I am everything but a plain teenager. I have been reading a bit and since you're bound to this castle, I thought maybe finding a way for you to break that part of it would be a good start." His attitude was making me not want to help him at all.

I opened the book to start reading it but the first page read like that of a mad man. His sentences didn't make sense and his words were all stuck together. I hoped other chapters would be clearer. Flipping through the book, I still didn't come up with anything substantial enough to start trying to help him. "Well, while you are looking for nothing I guess I can explain myself to you. When I was first locked in the cell you can imagine how angry I was, well, from that frustration and anger came a few tricks I had learned. Usually with curses there are not any positive things for the one that is cursed. That is why I seem like a vampire, but I do not have any of the extra talents they would have. The speed, strength, and devilishly handsome looks that a traditional vampire would have." I looked up at him as a smile pulled at my mouth. I was sure he was handsome before all this happened. His mother and father were pretty good looking from that dream thing I had, so it probably passed down. "You know looks aren't everything, I'm sure that's what the witch was trying to teach you. Did you ever use your looks against anyone while you were not cursed?" I deterred him away from the answers for a moment so that I could get a bit more of a clue about why he was really cursed since he said the book I had been reading was all a big lie anyways. "I guess you could say I did that. Maybe broke a few dozen hearts with my looks, and possibly had some people put to death because of theirs." My mouth was wide open in shock, what kind of person would put someone to death because of the way they looked; a mad man, that's who. "Wow, yeah you definitely deserved this curse. As of right now, I'm on the witch's side." I gave him a smug grin and looked back down at the book that was giving me nothing. "Well, I will have to change that. Anyways, I found this little trick I could do about a decade after I had been in there. If I thought about the places I had been in the castle for a moment, I could project a sort of shadow throughout the castle and it basically has the same silhouette as me, but it is just a shadow. That is what you saw that day, sometimes I let it run around without even realizing people down there could see it. You must have excellent eyesight for you to have seen it from the bottom of the hill." He shrugged his shoulders and I accepted his answer for the first question; he was right, my eyes sight was incredible. "I still have to clean this place up, so if you want, you can come around the castle with me while I clean, and you talk; sound good?" I closed the book and picked up the cleaning things I had left there, including the generator for the vacuum and stuff I had brought up here before all of this happened.

I started walking with the buckets and broom, thinking the front foyer would be a good place to start. Again. "The only answer I can think of for the Black family line question is that you truly are from the line. You said it was your mother's last name?"

I sat the buckets down and watched the dust fly around me. I didn't really know how to explain this. "My mother took my father's last name when they got together, they never actually got married, not to the government's standards anyways. When we were born, my mother gave us her last name instead of my father's. It was mainly because they were in hiding and that was because they were horrible people." I shrugged and picked up the broom, I needed all the cobwebs down from the ceiling before I did anything down there. "More horrible than me?" His simple question posed more in my mind. Because I didn't know what was worse, sentencing people to death because of the way they looked, or killing and raping for fun. "Honestly? I don't completely know all of what you did so I can't make that decision, but you're tied as of right now." I flipped the broom, so the bristles were facing the ceiling, dragging a chair over to the corner of the room, I got up on it and began swatting at the ceiling.

Dust, spider webs, and all sorts of gross things started falling on me and if I wasn't careful, they would fall into my mouth. I shook out my hair and clothes and tried to get everything off of me before I continued. "Well, I guess I will have to change your mind, that is how I will get the curse off of me right? I guess the reason you were picked was because of me. I lied when I said that I had been alone all these years because there is a guy that visits once a month and when he retires, he sends someone else. Well, this last one was supposed to find a new knight for me so that I was protected and not let out of the room, and five years ago I found you. There were issues a while back with finding an ancestor of yours, they declined the invitation and then the one after that and then it fell to you."

I stopped my coughing and gagging on what I hoped wasn't a spider to turn on the chair and look at him. Was he being serious right now? I patted my clothes down and shook out my hair, I was going to get this story without any distractions. "Why though? I mean I get the knight DNA and everything but why me, why did that key appear to me in my closet? Why did that guy show up at my door and offer me a freaking castle of all things? Just, why all of this?" I waved my hands around to show him what I was trying to talk about. "You moved to this country and this town five years ago, and on that day, you crossed the threshold to the boundaries of this town. I felt you here." He pointed to his chest where his heart would be. I rolled my eyes and got back on the chair to finish the dusting. "Just because you say things like that doesn't mean I'm going to swoon like the girls did in the 1600s. Try again, kid." I said to the guy that was three hundred years older than me.

I finished swatting around at the ceiling and started cleaning everything else in the room, leaving the floor for last. "I am not trying to make you swoon, or anything, I literally felt your presence when you entered the borders of the town. I woke up and I sent the man that came once a month for you, but you were too young at the time. So, I waited. I waited because through my own research it told me that if I found someone that woke me up like you did, then they could break the curse. You are the curse breaker. Whether you believe it or not because I have a connection with every knight there has ever been in your line, so long as they were in the boundaries of the town."

I took his answer into consideration and processed it through my head. Some things still didn't add up. "Where did your father hire the original knight from?"

He gave me a weird look but thought about it for a moment. "Asia, he had been intrigued with their style of combat and their pride in their work, when he searched for someone, they all recommended a single man. He hired the man and it went generational from that. The story you read did not tell you this? The name Black was given to him because my father wanted to protect him in this new world he was in. I think he would have been fine with his original last name, but I was locked in a closet, so." He looked away from me and now that I knew that bit of information, I thought I could process this a bit better. The book had told me that they changed the original knight's name because it would keep him safe. "Well, that would make more sense, seeing as I'm Asian, with a white person's last name... I guess I can get on board with this whole curse breaking thing. We'll need to make a list of everything you did wrong and go from there." I nodded my head in my own agreement. "I do not think there is enough paper and ink in the world." I couldn't tell if it was a joke or not, but I laughed regardless.

Halo of Gray

I looked around the front foyer and sighed, it actually looked good. Every inch was dusted and polished to a high standard, it took like six hours, but it was done none the less. I was talking with Cyrus at the beginning of the cleaning hour but since the sun came up, he hadn't been in the room. I followed the trail of dust in the air from where he most likely walked through and found him hiding in the kitchen. I looked around and found nothing out of the ordinary or out of place, so he was just sitting in here, like a statue. "Why did you leave the room? I finally finished, and it looks awesome. I can actually see the room for what it's worth." I sat a bucket of cleaning supplies down on the counter and watched him look up from his book. "It is the sun, if any of it touches my already frail and peeling skin, it will burn me. It is like a bath of acid. The witch made sure that if by some miracle I made it out of the room and then out of the castle, I would still be bound by the night. Not unlike a vampire." His crooked smile made me smile back at him, but I didn't have much time for niceties. "Okay, in my bag I have paper and pens to start your amends. We need to write down everything you did wrong before you were cursed, including what you did to the witch for her to double cross your father." I started searching through my bag when he spoke up. "What do you mean double crossed? My father hired her to curse me, he knew the whole time." I could see that he was getting upset and I wasn't sure what he would do if he got mad enough. "In the book I traded with Margaret, it said that your dad only wanted to scare you straight, so to speak. He didn't want her to actually curse you. But once she found out who she was supposed to be scaring, she changed her mind and double crossed your father. He was guilty after seeing your disfigurement and made that room downstairs for you. He wanted to keep the town and you safe by putting you away." I told him all I knew about the witch and her true plan, I was surprised he didn't know this. "He never told me anything about that. But it is not surprising, he did not talk or look at me after everything was said and done anyway. He was scared, I think." His sad eyes looked down at the table. I didn't know what it was like to have a good relationship with a parent, even for a little bit, and I knew he had one with both of his, before his mother passed away. "Maybe, we should cross off *forgiving your father* from the beginning of the list." I shrugged and offered the option, making a smile cross his face as he nodded his head in agreement. "Okay, we should start on the rest of the list but first," I walked quickly to the other room and grabbed something I had been meaning to talk to him about. I walked back to the kitchen and showed him what was in my hand. The shiny pair of scissors in my hand flashed in the light of the candles, lanterns in the room. "What do you plan on doing with those? Stabbing me? Because I have tried that, and it does not work." He stared at the scissors and then back to the counter while I walked in front of him. I hadn't been this close to him since he took that chunk out of my still healing neck. "Since you've been in there, you haven't had a proper haircut. Or bath, but we'll come back to that. May I cut your hair?" It's something that was bothering me, but I didn't want to just do it and then him get mad about it. That would be rude, plus I knew that I couldn't change much about him because of the curse but if he could peel his own skin off and pull out pieces of hair for the book, then I could chop off a few feet of hair. "Is it really that bad?" He picked up a lock of dark gray hair and sniffed it. The hair formed thick and thin dreads of dirty hair and I hoped these scissors would be enough. They were practically dreadlocks. "Maybe it's gotten a bit out of hand but it's also not its original color either, so maybe, shaving it all off would be best." He looked at me with an almost sad expression, he really liked his hair. "I can't give you your old hair back, but I can make it look decent until you have a bath and all that good stuff. I still need to clean up stairs, the dining room, the second foyer, and pretty much everything. But turn around and we can get this taken care of, at least."

He slowly did what I asked and turned around on the stool letting his back face me. I walked up to him and gently took large chunks of his dirty hair into my hand. Taking the scissors, I began to chop off his extremely long hair. The clumps of dirt and hair fell to the ground as I kept the length of his hair to at least the bottom of his ears.

I knew that back in his time they were used to longer hair and I didn't want to give him a buzz cut on his first haircut in three centuries. Cutting his hair took longer than I anticipated but at least he looked healthier. His natural hair came out even if it was still dirty, but there were no more clumps of anything in it at least. It was still dark gray and dirty at the roots, but the ends were at least hair and not clumps of anything.

I took a step back and admired my work, my half-assed work. With his hair floating around his head and over his ears, it looked more like a halo of gray than hair, it was so light and fluffy without all of those dreads weighing them down. "Does it look proper?" He asked while I got lost in watching it bounce around his ears with every little movement. It reminded me of Einstein's hair, or at least what photos of him looked like.

I forgot to answer him and instead of words, I sort of just mumbled something to him. His loud obnoxious laugh brought me out of my thoughts and I knew my face was as red as a tomato. I never got embarrassed, but I was right now, and I don't like it one bit. "Yeah, it looks fine. We need to get to work. Let's start that list." I walked back to the counter and pulled my pen out of the bag. "First dastardly deed?" I asked him without looking up. "There were so many, it is really hard to pick out the very first. Maybe getting mad for no reason at the staff and my nanny, perhaps all the pranks and jokes I pulled on them. When I grew up, I ended up putting most, if not all, of the staff and caretakers to death because of my arrogance." Okay, that was a good place to start. I started scribbling down what he told me, and he went on and on. This was going to be a long day.

Ball Point Pen

I started writing at the top of the page, but I couldn't shake the feeling of his eyes on me. I looked up and saw him dead on staring at the pen in my hand. When I looked at the normal blue shelled pen in my left hand, I wondered why he was staring at it so hard. And then it dawned on me. He had never seen a ball point pen.

I moved the pen left and then right and watched as his eyes watched the pen. It was amusing to say the least and when I was done having my fun, I put it down. "It's a pen, I know it might be strange to you, but it's been around for a while." I smiled and stifled a laugh that wished to mock him. "Where's the ink for it? Not having a feather or a thick handle to it is strange enough, but how do you write without ink?" His child-like wonder amazed me. I was never able to surprise anyone with anything that I had or did, and now here is this three hundred + year old guy being amazed and surprised by a pen of all things.

I put the pen out for him to grab and examine. "It has ink inside of it, and this tiny ball at the tip rolls it out as you write with it. Simple and fast." I put the pen back down in front of him as he kept staring at it. I reached in my bag for another one and started writing down all the things he did wrong in his first life.

I started writing while he examined the pen in wonder. He was sort of adorable when he saw something for the first time. Kind of innocent when you think about it. I looked down at the paper and then back at him and thought about something. "You know you should really be writing this. You know more than I do and I still need to get to the other parts of the castle and clean up a bit, so I can see what else this place has to offer. And maybe go to school tomorrow. Who knows?" I shrugged my shoulders and left the paper alone on the counter. "So, get to it and I'll see you when you're done." I smiled at him, trying to hold the pen the right way and before I laughed at him for actually acting adorable enough for me to take a bit of pity on him, I left the room. Deciding that the upstairs needed some love, I dragged the small generator and vacuum up the stairs along with the buckets of cleaning things I had laying around the castle like I owned it. *Oh wait, I guess I did own it.*

I thought about another passage I read in the book Margaret said she wrote, the one she traded me for. I remember briefly reading about a small loophole in the *being bound to the castle thing* and if I could think back hard enough, I might be able to remember it. I arrived at the top of the stairs and sat down the generator, vacuum, and bucket, before figuring out what room I would start with first.

I walked along the hallway walls and touched each door as I went. There were a lot of doors and rooms, and I figured if I cleaned the hallway first, it would be quicker and then the bedrooms another day. As I got closer to a certain door, I felt a sort of heat wave come over me, like I was on a beach in the middle of July. I could smell the warm sand and the feel of it between my toes. I had to shake my head clear of the sudden beach daydreams and went back for the rag to start dusting the walls and everything that hung off of them.

Time was passing by rather slowly even if I was keeping busy. I hadn't heard from Cyrus, so I was assumed he was still busy on his list. I looked out of one of the windows and saw that the sun was high in the sky, it was probably about noon. I wondered what I was missing in school today.

Finishing off the last of the knick-knacks and smaller stuff on the walls, I started back for the vacuum. Plugging the vacuum into the adapter on the generator, I started it up and began the grueling process of cleaning up after dead people, so I could actually see the place for what it should be.

I swept the vacuum over the carpet, picking up small crumbs and bigger ones like dead bugs and the webs they had been caught up in. I was getting into a grove when I got halfway down the hall and the weird sensation came over me again.

Feeling the warmth of the sun from inside a house was weird, especially in a place like this that was made of stone and had very little windows. I ignored the feeling once again and kept sweeping the vacuum over the carpet.

When I heard the faint sound of gravel being sucked up into the vacuum, I had to stop and make sure I wasn't sucking up something I shouldn't have been. When I looked down at the carpet everything looked normal, but when I squatted down and ran my hand over the threads of the fabric, I felt the familiar feeling of sand under my fingertips. Only I knew there wasn't a beach for miles around.

I ran the vacuum over it again, but it just seemed to keep coming out and onto the carpet. I looked up at the door that the sand seemed to lead to. It was a normal door in a normal abandoned castle, with normal sand coming out of it. Nothing could possibly go wrong if I just opened it to see what all the sand was about. Right?

I turned off the vacuum and stood in front of the door, preparing myself for whatever might be behind it. Grabbing the door knob and hoping I wasn't making it too obvious that I wanted there to be a massive beach connecting to a massive crystal blue ocean, but even I knew that would be a stretch. Turning the knob to the mysterious sand producing room, and when the door opened my mouth did too.

The scene before me took my breath away.

Tentacles and streams of gold and tan sand flew in a circular direction with multiple sections that tapered off into different sized circles around the room. It was filled with all these streams of magic sand and what else would I call it? This was truly magical.

I walked closer to the flying sand and lifted my hand to one of the streams. The sand was cold to the touch, unlike the feeling it gave me through the door. As I stepped closer into the room, I saw that the sand not only floated through the room but filled the floor of the room as well. I stepped through the near foot of sand that covered the floor. The mounds of sand covered my feet and it felt amazing, it had been so long since I went to the beach and I missed it in moments like this.

I got to the middle of the room and looked over the vibrant strands of sand weaving in and through the air of the room and when I looked over to the door, I saw Cyrus standing in its doorway. "You should not have come in this room."

His eyes flashed black and all the sand in the room seemed to stand still.

Like Rubbing Sand in Your Wound

Should I run? Should I try and reason with him in this state? Should I attempt to jump out of the window behind me? I mean it wouldn't be that far of a fall, no wait, I'm on the second floor, it would be a major fall. I'll just throw that plan away.

Several things ran through my head as his black eyes bore into mine, his temper flaring up and down as his concentration never wavered. For the first time since I opened that iron and silver door, his gaze made my skin shiver with fear, I hadn't felt a fear like this in a long time.

He slowly walked towards where I was standing, and the sand around me stopped all together, like it was waiting for his words to make it move again. The room grew colder and colder, like his body had absorbed all the heat in the room. The black in his eyes began to run down his face like tears, and again it looked like poison bleeding from his eyes. "This room is sacred, you should not have even been able to enter it." He stopped coming towards me and instead looked around at the streams of sand that were now frozen in the air around us. I held my breath for his next move. I inched closer to the stone wall behind me where the window was, I knew he wouldn't get close enough to me since the sun was still up so as long as I stayed in the sunlight, I was safe. "I apologize, but in my defense, you never told me of any rooms that were off limits, and I was only cleaning when this warmth fell over me. It was like the room wanted me to open its door and see what was inside." I scrambled for a plausible excuse to buy myself some time. "WHAT GIVES YOU THE RIGHT? This is my home and this room is… is special, what gives you the right to intrude on it? Have you no restraint?" His deep raspy voice rang through the room, making me physically flinch.

This was a side I hadn't seen of him yet, this was the prince before the curse, the one that was deserving. Not the one I was around a few hours ago, one that wanted to make amends and try to get his life back. As soon as the screaming was done, the black on his face stopped dripping and the black covering his eyes faded away. I stared at the red irises that I had grown to enjoy seeing, I loved watching his eyes, that was the first time I admitted that to myself.

His personality changed like the direction of the wind during a storm. A storm that I wasn't ready for and that could very well destroy everything in its path. He was a hurricane trapped inside flesh and bone. "I have restraint, but this room just called to me, this is your home I know, and I am sorry. However, it was left to me so technically it is my house, but I didn't want to step on your feet, so I didn't want to lay claim to it. But I will leave this one alone if that's what you want. I thought it was quite amazing, filled with all sorts of magic." There was a softness to my voice that I hoped he took as a sort of surrender.

He turned away from me and slumped his head down. He ran a hand over his face and massaged his temples like a headache was forming just under his mean demeanor. When he slumped over like that, we were basically the same height, which couldn't be good for his back now that I thought about it.

I breathed a bit easier when I saw his muscles relax more and his stance back down a bit, I didn't feel like he would attack me at any moment. He lifted his hand to the streams of sand above his head and when he did, the sand came to life and wrapped itself around his fingers. I watched the sand go in between each of his fingers weaving in and out like it was a sort of pet to him. "You were right about one thing; it is magic. It is the time I have spent in this castle and the time I have left. The witch cursed me and gave me a time limit, but it goes for an eternity, so I have no relief from death, the sand mocks me and my time on this Earth. That is something you will not read about in any book. I know eternity is a long time but every time a grain of sand fell to the ground around the streams, I felt it. Each and every one of them and as you can see the floor is swimming in the grains." He turned slowly back towards me, only his eyes held sadness in them and no danger. "That is where the pain comes from, the agonizing and constant pain that comes in waves. It was each grain of sand that fell, and over time, I got used to it but like the curse implied, as I got used to it the pain would change and it would make me feel again. It is never ending, and when you entered this room I felt it, it is connected to me in nearly every way. I could feel your hands run through the different streams, even the feelings you felt as you saw the sand for the first time." His eyes met mine and I realized that I felt vulnerable for the first time in front of him, for the first time in a long time.

He was now standing in front of me, his sultry words distracted me while he crept closer and closer, like he was trying to hypnotize me so that I didn't see him get closer, and closer. Until, the only room between us was the tip of our noses.

I hadn't realized that he wasn't that much taller than me, his nose only stopped just above mine, but only when he slouched over like he usually did.

I tried not to look at him, mainly because I wasn't sure what was going on anymore. He was mad, and then apologetic, and then… something else. Even my emotions and feelings were all over the place and I wasn't sure what it would land on. "It is all connected, Henrietta, and you are the final piece of the puzzle I have been looking for; the proof is in the sand. It called to you and allowed you in the room, and since you woke me from the prison cell I have not felt a single grain fall from its wandering height. You are the answer to the curse and it is time you broke it." His words felt good and I didn't think words have ever felt like this before.

I shook my head, he was playing games with me, he was getting in my head, and making me feel things I had been trying to repress, things that didn't need to be brought to light. I looked up at him and wondered why he thought he needed to be cured, as long as I could figure a way around him being bound to the castle and the whole sun thing, he could live a regular life. I wasn't needed in the slightest but here he was trying to use me; I hated being used.

There was something bugging me more than him trying to plan games with my head. "How did you know my name?" I asked him in a serious tone. "I knew the second you crossed into this town, you do not think I would not know every other detail about you?" That answer enraged me. I had had enough.

Lifting my hands to his chest and shoving him away quickly, I made my way out of the room and hurried towards the front door. He wasn't going to get inside my head anymore, I wasn't going to be his cure. I wasn't going to get close to him, help him from his curse, and then be thrown aside like garbage.

I left the castle in a huff and sped my way down to my house. I practically crashed into my front yard and ran to the door. I slammed my front door closed and then ran to the couch. I flung my tired body onto the cushions and gathered a pillow in my arms.

If he wanted me back in that castle, he was going to have to prove to me that I'm not just there to break his damn curse. I wasn't going to be used, abused, and then thrown away. Before my eyes closed in frustration and tiredness, I could have sworn I heard him yell my name from the castle walls.

Home Invasion

My body was stiff and from the angle I woke up in, I wasn't surprised. I was hunched over with my knees against my stomach and curled around the pillow. I guess I didn't realize I fell asleep where I crashed onto the couch yesterday.

I moved my stiff body into the upright position and stretched out my tired muscles. The small groan that came from my body made me realize I hadn't slept through the night like that in a while. It felt amazing.

I looked at the clock on the wall and saw that it was around six in the morning, what day it was I wasn't sure.

I regretfully got off the couch and dragged my legs up the stairs and into my bathroom for a much-needed shower. When I took a look at myself in the mirror, I saw that a lot of my color had come back and when I took the bandage off, the wound seemed nearly healed. There would be a wicked scar but at least I wasn't in danger of bleeding out anymore.

He still hadn't said sorry about that either.

I waved off my anger and got into the warm shower stream I had started when I got into the bathroom.

Quite literally jumping out of the shower and quickly wrapping my vastly chilling body in a warm fluffy towel, I stood in front of the mirror again. I wiped away the condensation from the surface and took my brush in my hand. Make a few quick strokes through my hair, I set it up to air dry like usual. I knew I needed to go to school today, I missed Wednesday, and I assumed Thursday. Which should make today Friday.

Olivia should be home today, and I hoped she didn't ask about the lovely souvenir I got, seeing as I didn't get her anything. Although, if I had told her like that, she would have laughed and then scolded me right afterwards. She was a great mother and role model but there were sometimes when she acted like a sister and just goofed around with me.

I flopped down on my bed and got a serious feeling of déjà vu. Shaking the feeling of doing my life over again, one scene at a time, I picked out what I wanted to wear to school.

I finished getting dressed and gathering my school supplies for the rest of the day. Looking at the clock, I had wasted a good hour getting ready and I needed to get going on my walk to death row, otherwise known as high school.

Closing the front door, making sure it was locked completely, I started down the path that would eventually lead me to the high school. As I walked, I wondered what my sister did over her little business trip and what time she would be back. I missed her like crazy but at the same time, we needed distance from each other, otherwise we would be at each other's throats.

I saw the high school come into view and I'd have to say my time away from it didn't done me any good; I still didn't want to enter those halls and I didn't want to listen to the teachers.

I knew I had left my current copy of *The Cursed Prince* at the castle, so I didn't have a book to get me by and I was too far past Margaret's book store to grab one real fast. I hadn't seen Margaret since she sprang the whole *I'm a four-hundred-year-old witch's* thing on me. I hoped she was okay.

Entering the halls of the school felt weird, like I didn't belong there anymore, like my life had become bigger than just going to school every day, graduating and then living a normal life. I felt like a door to the extraordinary had been opened for me and I forced it closed by coming into these hallways.

I took in a deep breath and walked to my locker. Grabbing what I needed for my boring classes, I headed out for a day of torturous lessons about stuff I already knew from being home schooled by my sister.

That was the other thing, while I didn't have time or resources to go to normal school growing up, my sister, being a genius, taught me while my parents were *out*. If I had tested to get into this school, I would have tested at a college level. But we needed to be *normal* or some BS like that. So, I sucked it up and now I was bored out of my mind every day.

I had finally got to the last class of the day, which happened to be the worst class. Math. Even with my sister being a genius, she still couldn't teach me to like math.

I had several teachers ask me to stay after school today to make up some tests I had missed, or whatever and since I wasn't planning on going to the castle today, I agreed. Now, I just had to get through math class.

Hearing the bell was music to my ears and as I headed to study hall for the tests I needed to make up, I realized I had never been to study hall. Finding it was harder than I imagined and sitting in the hard-plastic chairs was harder as well. I had three tests to make up along with a couple of assignments.

Trudging through the last of my paperwork, I could literally taste the freedom on my tongue; I wanted to go home so bad. I stood up with all the papers and handed them to the assigned teacher for the room. He gave me a nod and I was on my merry little way.

On the walk back to my house, I noticed the clouds were in abundance tonight and that usually meant night showers. I loved the rain at night, during the day it wasn't so great, dealing with mud and all that. But at night, I could enjoy it from my bedroom window and not have to deal with the mud.

I was nearly at my house when I looked up at the dark stone castle. From the outside you wouldn't expect there to be a three-hundred-year-old toddler living there and throwing tantrums every night. You wouldn't think I nearly bled out on the kitchen floor, the clean kitchen floor. You also probably wouldn't believe me when I said that there was a room filled with magic sand. Because from the outside, it looked like an abandoned castle.

Getting to my front door, I greeted it with a key and it responded by letting me into the house. The second I opened the door; however, I noticed a few things.

One, my sister's bag was lying on the couch along with her suitcase, but she was nowhere to be found.

Two, the TV was on and tuned to our favorite channel, but again she was nowhere to be found.

Three, the house was too quiet.

Four, there was these small drops of blood leading into the kitchen.

I held my breath because if it was who I thought it was then we were in trouble, but on another note, I was confused about, how they would have found us. We were so careful. I shook the thoughts about seeing my parents again and walked slowly to the kitchen. But all this was too familiar.

I placed my left palm on the revolving door in front of me and gave it a gentle push, mentally preparing myself for what was on the other side.

When the door came to a complete stop and the scene in the kitchen was laid out in front of me, I didn't even have time to gasp, because the air was taking out of my lungs faster than it could be replaced.

There in front of me and in the middle of my kitchen, stood Cyrus. He had his mouth dug into my sister's throat attempting to drain her dry. He suddenly came up for air and looked directly at me. Blood poured from his mouth with his razor sharp and pointed teeth that were stained with her blood.

He held her in place and looked me in the eye. His black orbs didn't go back to their usual color and I knew it was because of the blood. My sister's blood that was now dripping on the floor making a large puddle.

I started for her, but he clutched her to him tighter, warning me to stay away. "You left me, Henrietta. That was not nice. Come back to the castle with me and your sister is only left with a scar, instead of the crater where her head is now."

I knew he meant what he said, and I knew I would go with him for her sake. But I also knew that I didn't take orders from anyone. Not even a fucking prince.

Loophole

His anger was coming off in waves and I knew if I didn't go with him, he would kill Olivia. All I wanted was her safety. I wasn't going to surrender though, I was going to make a deal. "Cyrus, you will not do a single thing more to her. You've said it yourself, you need me. So, you wouldn't want to harm the only person in this world I love, right? Just sit her down on the floor and let me tend to her wound, then I will go with you. No more hissy fits." I stared him dead in the eyes and watched as the black faded and drained from them, replacing it with a deep red.

He closed his mouth and wiped some of the blood away from his lips. His grip on my sister's throat loosened and before she hit the floor, I jumped to catch her, making me land on my knees, hard.

I quickly pushed her up into a sitting position and leaned her against the wall. I lifted her head and made her look at me, she was completely unconscious and by the color of her skin, he had taken too much. I didn't want to leave her here, but I needed to bandage her up and leave a note, so she didn't think I just ran away, or that something worse happened.

I quickly ran to the cabinet and got the spray, bandages, and a towel to wipe up some of the blood. I sprayed her neck and wiped up some underneath the wound. She was lucky it wasn't oozing anymore, which wasn't always a good thing. I sprayed a bit more and covered it with a thick piece of gauze and then taped it up properly. Given time and rest, her blood should replace itself and then she'd be fine. She should go to the hospital, but I knew if she woke up there, she would never forgive me; she absolutely hated hospitals. She even had reoccurring nightmares about them.

I grabbed her under the arms and started to drag her from the kitchen to the living room when an arm stopped me. I looked up at him and all he did was shake his head. "I'm just taking her to the living room, so she doesn't wake up on the ground. You can wait a few minutes." I wasn't having anymore of his BS; he was acting like a child, so I was going to treat him as such.

I dragged her body and heaved her onto the couch, making sure she was comfy before I ran away to the castle. I brushed her hair out of her eyes and kissed her forehead telling her in her ear, that I would be back before she knew it.

I headed back to the kitchen and scribbled out a quick note. Motioning for the toddler to follow behind me, we headed for the front door. I stopped by my scooter and wondered if he would sit on the back, or if he was going to walk. I strapped my helmet onto my head and pulled my scooter up into the upright position. Taking a seat and straddling it between my legs, I waited for him to notice I wasn't walking behind him.

He stopped when he came to the sidewalk and looked back only to not see me standing behind him like the sheep he wanted.

I motioned for him to come over to me and sit on the back of the scooter; I was growing impatient. He wanted me back at the castle then I would go, but I would do it my own way. He looked down at my bumble bee yellow scooter and then to me. He had an expression that I could only assume mean *you've got to be kidding*. "Get on or walk, it's not going to bite you." I joked around but I wasn't in the mood for his attitude anymore tonight. He had pissed me off enough.

He swung his leg over like I had and took his seat behind me. I knew he was uncomfortable, but I couldn't care less right now. I started the scooter up and started to pull out of the front yard. I felt his hand tighten around my shoulders and I smiled to myself, I was actually able to instill a bit of fear in the big bad monster.

The ride took longer than usual, mainly because I had to shove his hands off me every now and then with my shoulders because of his iron grip which made me slow down a bunch. I stopped the scooter and he was off it, in nothing flat. If I didn't know any better, I would have guessed he was scared.

I followed behind him and entered the castle as he did. We got to the first foyer when he stopped walking. I threw the bag I had snagged from the living room before we left and let it fall to the floor. "What's your fucking issue? You can't stand to be alone? What did you do all those years by yourself in that prison cell? Why the hell would you attack my sister, the only person I care about and love? If you would have waited, I might have come back on my own accord!" I was screaming at him, face red, arms flailing, and all.

He looked at me with a stone-cold face, like he didn't care about what he did. "Why would you give up your life at home with your sister just to come here with me? I mean I know I threatened her but you could have still fought to stay there." I could not believe what he was saying, he was going to make me go insane, I just knew it. "Did you think you gave me an actual choice here, you were going to kill her if I hadn't told you I would come to the castle? That's what you do for the people you love, you sacrifice your own happiness for them. Maybe that's why you're cursed, you can't think of anyone but yourself." I spat at him in my rage then walked off my anger and went to the kitchen. "How did you leave the castle?" I had to change the subject because if I didn't, I would have taken a knife to his throat and all it would do would make a mess because he couldn't die, that was the curse. And that's something I didn't feel like cleaning up. "You left your lovely book here and I gave it a read. There was a loophole, it said, *the cursed could not leave the premises of the castle*. So, I took this with me." I watched as he pulled a brick that I assumed came from the castle walls and showed it to me. "And I sniffed out your scent. I found your house and your sister came in; she surprised me. Her scent was similar to yours and it reminded me of the day I attacked you. I could not help myself." He took a seat in front of me at the counter and I looked into his eyes. "You could have helped yourself, you could have not drunk my sister's blood. You could have not threatened me. How do you ever expect to break your curse by not changing your ways?" I thought I actually got to him this time because the look that crossed his face could have only been seen as guilty.

This was a start.

Mirror Mirror

The last time I was on my hands and knees scrubbing up something on the floor I was eight and I had dropped a plate of mac and cheese, and I needed to get it cleaned up before my parents got home. The only reason I was scrubbing the floor right now with my bare hands and a rag was because I forgot the mop at home. I moved the scrub brush back and forth over the stone floor and watched the soapy bubbles foam up and then float into the air around me and pop in midair. I was still at the castle and this time, I decided to take on one of the many bathrooms just, so I could see what they were supposed to look like, the other ones could wait for whomever bought this place from me.

I stood up and looked around at my progress and the bucket of soapy water that was half full now. I moved on to the counters and scrubbed them clean, I was waiting to do the bathtub last, seeing as it was the dirtiest. I looked over at the grime filled tub and sighed, I really hated cleaning, and if I didn't want to resell this place in the end, I wouldn't be doing any of this.

The only things I had done since taking this piece of crap they call a castle, was clean a few rooms and let something out that I probably shouldn't have.

I heard a knock at the door and knew it would be him. I wondered who I needed to talk to for the babysitting job I unwillingly took, because it didn't seem like I would get paid for it. I rolled my eyes at the unopened door and then walked to open it. Standing on the other side was none other than Cyrus himself. He looked at me and then at the room behind me like he hadn't seen a bathroom before. "What do you need? I said I would come back to the castle, not be around you twenty-four seven. Let me be." I was about to close the door on him, when

94

he stopped it with his hand. "I was wondering if you could help me with something, and it is hard for me to ask… so this may take a while." I glared at him and opened the door again, waiting for his long question.

He stood there and fidgeted with his hands and rocked back and forth on the heel of his feet looking like he was trying to buy time. "Okay, you stand there and think about your question while I clean the tub." I turned away from him and picked the bucket back up. Walking to the tub, I picked up the tub stopper and plugged it into the drain. Lifting the bucket, I dumped the soapy water into the gross tub and began the scrubbing.

On my knees again, scrubbing the sides of the tub and reaching into the bottom to get the grime down there as well. I wiped my forehead with a free hand and looked up to the door at Cyrus who was supposed to be asking me a question. I looked at him only to see him watching me clean the tub. "Have you gained any more confidence yet? Are you ready to ask me that question that seems to be at the front of your mind?" I spoke to him while I drained the tub of the now gross soapy water. I grabbed a squirt bottle and wiped down what didn't drain down the tub. "What I want to ask is embarrassing and I do not want you to laugh. But I would like your help… running a… a bath for myself. I have… I have never…" I stopped scrubbing and spraying to look up at him and his fumbling words. "You have never… what? Ran a bath for yourself?" I watched as he shook his head in a slow yes and I gave him a shocked expression back. "You're kidding, you've never made a bath for yourself?" If his skin color could change, it would be bright red with embarrassment. "I always had a maid or nannies draw one for me, and now that it has that weird shiny thing on it, I have no clue how to work it." He threw his arms up in a huff and then crossed them in defeat.

I had to keep telling myself that he got me back here by threatening my sister's life and that he wasn't supposed to look like a lost puppy. But I was having a hard time. "It's called a waterspout and it's where the water comes from. Usually from a well, or the city's water line. The knobs turn it hot, or cold and that's about it. I guess if you want I'll fill the tub for you, but you can do the rest, you're a three hundred and seven-year-old man, you can bathe yourself." I stood up with help from the now clean tub and started the water at the faucet.

I turned it on nothing but hot with a bit of the cold on as well. I cleaned up my supplies and walked them to the hallway while I waited for the water to reach the line. I wasn't sure how the water was getting hot since there wasn't any electricity, but I wasn't that curious. Maybe there was a gas line running into the castle now, maybe that's something I should look into.

I waited until the water reached the peak of its fill and then let a bit of the soap go into the water creating bubbles. I turned off the water and walked back to Cyrus in the doorway. "Alright, it's ready, I assume you know what to do from here, right? I put some more soap for your hair and everything next to the tub. Have fun." I wiggled my eyebrows at him and laughed at his confused face. I walked out of the room and closed the door for him. I might as well go clear out a room for me to sleep in, since I was going to be castle bound for god knows how long.

After a while of clearing out some of the dusty things from a random bedroom, I heard Cyrus call my name. Being the curious kitten, I am, I decided to go see what he wanted. I got to the bathroom door and gave it a loud knock and in a moment, it was flung open to a very wet and towel covered Cyrus. I looked at his face and saw that he was very upset. I lowered my knocking fist and waited for him to speak up. "I cannot see, it is like there is nothing there!" His voice went from low pitched to high and he seemed to stay in his freaked-out position. "Do you mean that you can't see me right now, like you've gone blind?" I asked the most obvious question and got the sourest look back. "NO! I mean the mirror, I cannot see myself in the mirror!" He walked to the mirror and motioned for me to follow him into the steam filled bathroom.

He wiped the mirror for what looked like the second time and stood in front of it. "See, there is nothing there. Just a blank space, like I am invisible…" I investigated the mirror like he was and saw the same thing. Nothing. "It's probably part of the curse, like a vanity clause, or something. The witch obviously didn't want you to see yourself either. If it helps any a lot of the dead, peeling skin has come off since your bath. But your skin and hair color are the same. Gray." I spoke cautiously around him because even if I was mad at him right now, it didn't mean that I wanted him to think he was ugly or something. "I hate this curse, I used to be so handsome, and now I have gray hair like an old lady and peeling skin like a dead person. And I cannot even complain about it to the mirror." He touched his face and tried to look at himself in the mirror again. "Oh, stop throwing a fit, you look fine. When the curse is gone you'll be back to your pompous and vain self. Don't worry." I didn't stick around to see his expression, or for him to say anything. He was being a baby again and I had other things to do.

Shopping Bender

I threw myself on the old bed that was naked without all the covers which were currently soaking in the now clean bathroom. I would have to wait until I rinsed them and hung them out to dry and then I would be able to curl up in a big blanket. There was no way I was going to lay on blankets from hundreds of years ago, not without washing them.

But while I was laying down on a big beautiful bed in a big beautiful castle, I still wasn't happy. I hated seeing Cyrus look so down about how he looked, I knew what it was like to have poor or no self-esteem, I had never heard the word *I love you* until my sister uttered it one day, or the words *you're beautiful* until my first day of real school, again from my sister. I knew he hated what the curse did to what he used to look like and I knew he wanted to look the way he used to, but I couldn't do anything for him right now.

I sat up from the bed rather quickly, I think I had an idea. But I would need to talk him into letting me leave for a few hours. Maybe if I told him I would bring him back a toy he would let me, that usually worked on me when we first moved here, and my sister would have to go on her business trips without me. "Oh Cyrus... Could you come here for a second?" My new live-in roommate heeded my call and dragged himself to my temporary room.

He leaned against the door frame and crossed his arms, like it was such a task for him to come when I called. I rolled my eyes for the millionth time today at him as he just kept standing there. "You wanted something?" His low voice answered my call before I had the chance to ask him a question. "I would like to go out, to the store, by myself. It won't be long, and I promise I'll bring you something back." I used my puppy dog eyes and my pouty lip to get what I wanted, and I hoped it worked.

I watched him close his eyes and I assumed he was counting to ten so that he wouldn't get mad at me for wanting to do something without him. Or maybe that was just his thinking face. "You know I think after all those years of being in that room I may have heard that they make chocolate in a bar now. It used to be so rare when I was… not cursed… and if they make it by the bar now then that is what I want. Chocolate. I really hope I can eat it and all, I would like to try anyways. But please be quick, this castle is quite lonely without you roaming the halls, with your attitude and cleaning products." I think my face cracked a smile at something he said. "Well, I'll try and keep the attitude to a greater height when I return." I stood up from the bed with every intention of leaving right then and there. I grabbed my small backpack from the ground and heaved it over my shoulder.

I passed him by through the doorway, he didn't even move out of the way. I knew he thought I would go by and see if my sister was okay, but I also knew that he needed to trust me just as I needed to trust him for any of this to work, for us to figure out the curse; this was my starting point. "I'll be back soon, don't kill any villagers while I'm gone." I waved my hand as I walked towards the door and then to the twenty-four-hour grocery store.

I walked out of the castle without getting another word from him. The store wasn't on my route for the house and I knew I wouldn't go there; it could put her in danger. Plus, it would be a big waste of time. I knew that she would be okay, she's been through worse and seen worse, that's why she was shy and skittish now. I dropped a book once and she yelped like I had hit her. Some days it was like being around an abused dog. It was a wonder how we turned out so differently, but still damaged at the same time.

The walk to the store was nothing, I knew I wouldn't need my scooter for it either, plus I liked walking so early in the morning. Seeing the store in the distance, I quickened my pace a bit. After entering through the door with the sound of a bell, I made my way towards the aisle I needed. Now for this to work, I would need two different ones… When I got to the aisle, I picked up the two boxes I would need and then I headed to the checkout counter.

When I got to the belt for the checkout, I realized I had forgotten about the chocolate bar for Cyrus. I sat the stuff down and ran to the candy aisle and stopped when I saw all the different kinds of chocolate. I ran my eyes over the hundreds of choices and I realized I hadn't bought candy in a long time because here were so many new things out now.

I didn't know if I could pick just one and I knew he wouldn't just be going out for candy all willy-nilly, maybe I should just take a little of everything. Call it a chocolate bender if you will. Arms filled with chocolate bars, I spilled them out on the conveyor belt along with the other stuff I had left there when I ran back for the chocolate. The middle-aged lady rung up my till and spilled out the price for it all. I gave her the cash and took the couple of bags it all fit into and headed out.

I had the bags hanging from my arms as I walked and honestly, I think I was more excited about the chocolate bars and his expression when I gave them to him than the other stuff I got. I hoped just like him, that he could eat them too. He had told me at one time that he couldn't eat regular food, but chocolate may not count. I guess we'd find out.

The trip back to the castle was shorter since I was so excited, even the large door didn't bother me as I stormed through them.

I walked quickly through the foyer and then met the staircase with my sneakers. Going into a light jog up the stairs I made it to my temporary room in nothing flat. I was giddy with excitement and since I hadn't seen Cyrus yet, I decided to go and do the first part of my surprise before he realized I was back. I dumped the chocolate on the bed and then headed to the bathroom with the other part of the purchase.

I wasn't sure how long I had been in the bathroom but keeping my hair wrapped in a towel until it dried and getting back to the bedroom, I noticed the sun was bright and shiny. Opening the bedroom door, I saw that Cyrus had found the chocolate bag. "I think you bought the whole store. I did not know they made so many things out of chocolate." His eyes were wide like a child in a literal candy store. "That's not even half of it, it was just the pure chocolate bars. Just wait until you have the ones with nuts, and krispies in them." I walked towards the bag on the ground and grabbed the hat out of my bag. Going on the other side of him so that he didn't see, I flipped my hair out of the towel and wrapped it up inside the beanie hat.

I walked around the other side of the bed and joined him there with the candy. "Are you going to eat a piece?" I asked him while he just stared at the chocolate bars. "It is a bit intimidating, all this chocolate. I think I have eaten a single piece in my whole existence. Now there is just so many, it is hard to choose." I picked up a regular Hershey's milk chocolate bar to start him off, I wasn't really into the chocolate in the UK because it was a lot more bitter than the chocolate in America. Peeling the wrapper off and popping off a piece, I handed him a square and watched him pop it into his mouth.

The look on his face was priceless. It was pure joy and amazement, and totally worth buying nearly all the chocolate in the place, just to see his face like this. It was something I could get used to, if he kept it down.

Graveyard Shift

"Are you ready?" I asked him as sweetly as I could. "No." He told me with a grumble. "Are you sure you're not?" I sang next to him. "NO, I do not want to go, and I am opposed to being forced!" He actually stomped his foot in defiance. "Stop being a child and just come on! It's crucial to your healing." Using hand gestures and everything, trying to get him to bundle up and come outside with me.

I huffed and puffed and tried to get the toddler to go to the graveyard with me, but no, he wanted to throw a fit. I rolled my eyes at him and put my jacket on. It was either late Friday night, or early Saturday morning, I wasn't completely sure at the moment. All I knew was that it was chilly outside, and I didn't want to catch a cold. "Why do we have to start my amends there though?" He stomped his foot and crossed his arms. "Because most of the bad that you did, including sentencing people to death and any others you may have killed by your own hand or even just didn't like, are buried in the town's cemetery. So, you are going to go down there and tell them you're sorry. And you'll mean it." I found that more and more I sounded like a mother instead of a teenager. What was this guy doing to me? I slowly lowered my pointing finger as I tried to talk him into going with me. "It will not work if you MAKE me do it." He was right, of course, but I wouldn't let him know that. "Exactly, I'm hoping that seeing their tombstones will instill a bit of remorse in your cold heart and then we can begin your healing." I played the plan off cool and hoped he would just go along with it.

I watched his expression turn from one of annoyance at leaving the castle, to one of brooding agreement. I'll take it. I gave him a nod and then turned towards the front door. I listened to his footsteps follow after me and before we left the castle completely, I needed to get one thing.

I turned and faced the stone of the castle walls. I had put back the one he took when he left the first time, so I wouldn't have to chisel a different one out. Counting the rows out loud, I pinpointed the one that I needed. Grabbing a hold of it and giving it a bit of a wiggle, I had the stone out of its hole in the wall.

Walking back to Cyrus, who was stuck in the doorway by the unseen force that kept him bound to it, I tossed him the stone and like the flick of a switch, he was able to move out of the door's way. I was still unsure how he got it out the first time, maybe he stretched?

He held the stone like it was his lifeline, and it might as well be, who knew what would happen if the stone wasn't on his person suddenly. Would he get sucked back to the castle in a weird vortex thing? Or like disintegrate or something? The book didn't prepare me for this.

We started off in a silent walk towards the graveyard grounds. It was not too far from the castle seeing as it had the royal crypts in it. I had no idea what brought me to the conclusion that he should go and apologize to a bunch of grave markers, but I felt like it was the right thing.

It was supposed to be a nice warm night seeing as it was close to the end of the school year, but we had been getting unseasonably cold weather for this time of the year. I had to clutch the thin jacket I wore to keep warm, I knew he would be fine since he had told me previously that the weather never bothered him, not anymore.

It was in no time that we had gotten to the gates of the graveyard and by the look on his face, this place had changed a lot since he had last seen it. "When did you see this place last?" I asked him as I pried open the iron gates. "I was a boy and it was my – I mean, someone's funeral. It has grown since then. Immensely." He looked over all the stone graves, some gray and some black, his eyes never left them. I knew this would be hard for him, hell it was hard for me. Granted, I usually found graveyards peaceful, but tonight was different.

We entered further into the graveyard's grounds and something about the chill in the air made things just a bit creepier. I crossed my arms against my chest and watched as he walked in front of me, stone clutched in his hand like a safety blanket. He walked to different graves and looked at each one, I assumed he was thinking if he knew them or not. "The older people are in the back near the royal crypts. We should start there." I told him as I held my shakes of cold to myself.

He walked slowly towards the back of the yard and as he did, I wondered why he tried to cover up the funeral he was at the last time he was here. Maybe I should try and pull it out of him… Because I knew about it already, so he wasn't keeping anything from me, but I knew he thought I didn't know and I knew he didn't want me to know. "So, about that funeral you had been to before." I wasn't a very smooth talker, but I got the job done, eventually. "I do not wish to talk about it." His voice was straight and cold, but I wasn't done pushing for the answer I already knew. "Talking about it could be a key to helping you. How bad could it have been?" In a flash he was in front of me, staring me down with his cold, unforgiving eyes. I had to keep telling myself this wasn't a mistake, this was for the good of his healing. I just didn't know when to shut up sometimes. "Just talk to me. What's the worst that could happen?" I wasn't asking him, it was a rhetorical question. "I–I just… It is hard for me, it was the first devastating day that I really had as a child. I cannot talk about it, but maybe I could show you instead." He turned to me and started reaching for my arm.

I pulled back suddenly, not really loving the fact of anyone reaching for me with their hands, it's nothing personal, I just didn't like being touched. "What do you mean, show me?" I asked him as his hand hovered in the air, waiting for my approval and for my arm back. "The day you opened that prison door you saw a vision, yes?" I nodded my head and he continued. "It is part of my punishment, I am set to relive all of my most happy and devastating memories all at once. Trying to make me go mad with all the things I had done wrong in my life and all the bad things that happened to me. This one was particularly painful, and you are right, it was one of the first triggering things for me when it came to my downfall." His honesty was shocking but at the same time, I was happy he is opening up more to me.

I just wasn't sure about *'time jumping'* again, even if it's a memory, the last time it happened it was a weird trip. Like a vivid acid trip down memory lane. I guess if he could trust me by telling me about what happened to him, then I could trust him enough to let him show me. Here goes nothing.

Memory Pain

My hand was steady as I reached out to his outstretched one. I wasn't sure what would happen this trip around, but I hoped, no I knew that it would put him on the right path to figuring all this drama out. Let's do this.

Cyrus

She clutched onto my hand and I let her mind meld with my own like the first time her eyes had met mine. Her hand was cold, and I knew it was because of the weather, mine was because I had not had warmth flow through me in a long time.

When the painful memory hit my mind as if on cue, I let it run through both of our minds and in seconds, we were whisked away.

It was swirls of colors and shapes that did not belong. Usually these visions came in a snap and not a swirl, but this was not just my mind going through this memory. I had her mind melding with mine and these colors must be coming from her. The feel of her mind with mine felt familiar and like it had always been like this, but I digressed.

The swirls of colors stopped and with a flash of a brighter light, the scene before me changed into one from my childhood. I saw Henrietta standing next to me but when I tried to speak, my voice was silent. I touched my throat and realized that she did not even know I was next to her. Nor could she talk to me.

Personally, I had never walked through my visions like this, she has, this time she had the upper hand. I watched as she took the lead on finding the source of this particular vision. I followed her.

We were in the castle now and as I followed her I knew exactly where we were headed. When she stopped at the bedroom door of my childhood room, I waited for her to enter. I watched the door close without me on the other side of it. I was too much of a coward to go in there, I never could face this memory.

But I would do it for her.

I swallowed my fear and pushed the door open and followed her suit. When the door opened, I saw her standing in front of a young boy sitting on a bed. I looked around the room and saw that it was much too big for him and his size, something to grow into perhaps. My head throbbed with the truth about the scene in front of me. I knew who that was standing in front of her and why he was so upset and in a room that did not suit him, but I was trying to ignore it.

I stood in front of the child like she had been doing and when I saw the boy, I was brought back to what I had looked like as a small boy. Watching myself stare at the wall behind us, as if he was just looking through our bodies. He was sad and had tears streaming down his face. This was extremely hard for me and I knew it would be good but at the same time, I wanted to run for the hills.

I needed to stop wanting to run from all the bad things that happened to me and own up to them instead, and I hated to admit it but she was right; this was my start.

Me being angry all the time back then might be an understatement, I was a monster towards everyone and I still had not learned anything from it, the road in front of me was harder than I expected, granted I had never thought I would be doing something like this with someone like her but who was to say that the way she wanted to do things was not the right way? I had a lot of changes to make and I hoped she was there for every second of it.

I looked over at Henrietta only to see her face lined with tears as well, she was sad for my younger self. But why? Why would anyone want to help such a pathetic child like I had been?

Before my next thought, we both swung our heads to the door that was opening to reveal an old nanny of mine. In just a few years she would be dead and that would be my first real kill. Whether I had sentenced her, or if it was by my hand. In all honesty, I did not remember which one I had sentenced and which one I had poisoned.

My eyes went back to the younger form of myself and watched his attention turn to the large woman entering his room. "Young Prince, it is time." The woman told him, and he did as she asked. The younger me took her hand and walked with her outside the room.

I looked over and watched Henrietta follow after the both of them, curiosity showing all over her face. I knew she was enjoying seeing what my life was like before. She had told me before that she was a bookworm, which she then explained to me that that meant she loved to read. Whether it was about a different universe or the same one with a different spin. Which is why she liked walking through the castle so much and learning about my past. She reminded me of my mother.

We followed the younger version of myself and the nanny out to the graveyard grounds like we had just been at before. When we hit the outside of the castle, the weather changed drastically then what we had been in before.

Large chunks of white snowflakes were falling from the sky above us, blanketing the ground below our feet. I was uncertain if Henrietta liked the snow or not, I was not sure about a lot of what she did and did not like. I knew she did not like most of me. There were times, of course, that I would see her smile at something I said, but there were more times than not that I saw a frown or a scowl at something I did. Or, of course, when she rolled her eyes at my antics, which I knew was a sign of annoyance.

Sometimes, I was not sure what she did not like that I did, then there were other times where I saw very clearly what I had done to her. Sometimes, it was easier to be cruel towards her than nice.

She walked towards the crowd that was now forming around a specific area of the graveyard. I followed the crowd and her, not really wanting to relive this memory for the millionth time.

I took a step forward from where I stood and came up to Henrietta's shoulder, she was much shorter than I was. I was even able to see the top of her head with her normally black hair that was still covered by that weird head cover thing. I think she called it a beanie? Anyway, the scene before us had two coffins sitting in front of the crowd of people with my father at the front of them.

The nanny had brought the child version of me out to my father and the child's presence had gone unnoticed by the royal asshole. I saw Henrietta look at the coffins and then at the little boy. She noticed the special arrangement of the coffins and how one was a lot bigger than the other.

The one on the right was regular size and made of a special marble that would later be moved into the family crypt, the other one however was much smaller. It was the perfect size for an infant.

She walked closer to the coffins and listened to the priest speak for the dead and the living standing around him. She walked to the small boy and crouched down to his level and whispered something in his ear. If I could concentrate enough, it was like I could almost feel the warmth of her breath on my past self.

The moment she stopped talking to the boy, the swirls of color began again, and we were back in the dark and breezy graveyard of the present. "Your mother died that day, didn't she?" I looked over to her with her head hanging low, staring at the stone in the ground that represented my mother's grave even though the coffin was in the crypt. "Yes, she died a few days after my sister was born." She looked up to me and then down at the stone that was next to my mother's. "Was she sick?" A simple question that held such meaning. "No, my sister passed away after a few hours of being born. My mother could not take the pain of losing her first daughter. She took her own life, and I was the one who found her dead in her bedroom." For once, the tears that came from my eyes were not from physical pain, but from sadness, painful all the same. "I'm so sorry, that's a horrible kind of pain, especially at such a young age. What was your sister's name?" I knew she was trying to change the subject a bit and I went with it for her sake. "Delilah. Delilah Victoria Cross. She lived for nearly two hours. I never got to see her face, she was already wrapped in a black burial blanket." I stood over her gravestone wondering what she would have been like if she had lived. "By the way, what did you whisper in the boy's ear in the vision?" Curiosity had always been a problem for me. "I told him that he needed to be strong and one day he would meet a really awesome person that would take him to see everything the world has to offer. I knew he wouldn't be able to hear me, but it made me feel better."

She shrugged her shoulders and turned away from me.

She was right though, I did meet an amazing person and if this all worked out, I would make sure she kept that promise.

Just Like You

I sat in the bathtub that was closest to my new bedroom, I had just finished cleaning it and decided to take a bath. I leaned my head back and rested it on the edge of the large copper tub. If there was one thing I really loved about this place, it was the bathtubs.

I had let my hair down and finished the last part of my surprise. I had to wait an entire month for this last step and it was finally ready.

Yeah, a month was a long time to wait for, well anything, but it was going to be worth it. I thought back to the last few weeks of pretty much being trapped here and found it to be more boring than exciting. I guess when I agreed to come here until he was healed, I thought it would be more exciting, but it wasn't.

It had been a few weeks since he let me into his memory of being at his mother and sister's funeral and since then, I'd just been cleaning the castle. He'd been brooding and keeping to himself since then. I hoped the idea I had would work and bring him back out of the shell he'd been building around himself this month.

I blew on a small mound of bubbles that were floating on my belly making them fly all over the room, popping in the air. I loved bubble baths and I was so happy I had the time and energy to take a bath in this amazing tub.

Before the water got too cold, I scooted my butt down the tub and laid back in the frothy bubble filled water. Taking in a quick breath I dunked my head under the water of the deep, deep tub. I swished my hair around under the water and ran my hands through it, getting all the soap out of it. I always loved the feeling of my hair underwater, I didn't like the tangled mess it became afterwards.

Coming up for air, I slicked my hair back allowing the water to run off my head. I grabbed the edges of the tub and rubbed the copper edge with the pad of my thumb. It was weird, having a copper tub, it must have been put in after Cyrus had been cursed and everything. Mainly because this was a rare form of bathtub for that time. I knew the faucet and stuff was put in later because they most likely filled it in with buckets of hot water or something.

Thinking about what they used so long ago made my head hurt. I usually liked learning about things from the past, but I just didn't feel like thinking about anything, but my new plan to get him to put his life back in order.

I was still annoyed at the fact that he still had a long way to go and that I would be stuck here until everything panned out. I didn't know how long that was going to take either, I had no ideas on how to break this thing and I didn't think that one would pop into my head anytime soon.

I looked at the pads of my fingers and decided it was time to get out, I was all prune and the water was getting cold.

I stood up carefully in the tub and steadied myself with the walls of it as well. Stepping out of the copper bathtub, I reached out for the towel I had left on the counter in front of me. I wrapped it around my body and when I looked into the mirror and lead my eyes down my neck and on the scar that was in place of the gash that he had left behind.

I tried to not hold that against him, he was in an animalistic state of mind and he hadn't had anything to eat in a few centuries that would make anyone mad. But I wasn't forgiving him, not in the least. He was going to pay for the scar that will be on my neck for the rest of my life, but at least I was at the bottom of the amends list, there were others that needed to come first.

I towel dried my hair and the rest of my body. Getting into my night shirt and shorts that I had decided to wear even if it wasn't night time. I wasn't going to care about the way I dressed anymore, if I wasn't going to be going out of the castle very often, or at all anymore.

I looked at myself in the mirror again, only this time I ran my fingers through my wet hair trying to brush it as much as possible. I parted it the way it was supposed to be and looked at the finished product in the mirror. I hoped this worked, I wasn't too sure on any more ideas. Except for maybe more chocolate, he did love the chocolate. We were both happy that he was able to keep that down, weren't sure why, but we were happy about it.

At the end of my last thought, a knock came from the other side of the door.

Well, the only other person that could be was his royal brooding-ness, Prince Cyrus. I walked to the door after cleaning up a bit around the counters. I opened the door so that just my face peaked through the entrance, I didn't want the surprise to come early.

I looked up at him and his towering height and he down at me. I'm almost certain that I looked like a mouse trying to get out of a hole at the moment. "I was wondering if you had any more of the chocolate bars left in your room. And I guess that I am also sorry for staying away from you and our work for nearly a month." I stood up a bit straighter and looked at him better. I could have sworn, he rolled his eyes at me, but it could have been just the lighting. "Well, apology accepted and yes I have more in the room, but I have something to show you before you get a sugar high again." He nodded his head and I slipped my face back into the bathroom. I closed the door and readied myself for the big reveal.

Clutching the door knob and giving it a jerk of a twist, I swung the door open to face him full on.

I watched his eyes go from my face to my hair and widen in surprise. I knew he probably didn't know how I did it and I think that might be my favorite part of the whole thing. "What did you do to your hair?" He asked me with curiosity in his voice. "Well, a few weeks ago I lightened it, well bleached it, and then I had to wait for a while to do the rest of the dying. I dyed my hair. It's gray and it matches yours, now you don't have to be the only one with, what you call, ugly hair." I gave him a smug smile and rocked back and forth on the balls of my feet waiting for his response. "I will ask you how you did this later but for now I have to say, the color suits you well. Much more than it suits me. Also, thank you, for making me feel less cursed even if it was just for a moment." I knew he meant what he was saying, and I loved every second of it, because if he could forgive his father, apologize to me, and thank me for something as small as this, then we could get this curse lifted.

I had no doubt about it.

Eye Spy

"What does this one do?" Cyrus asked me as he held up another card towards me. "You aren't supposed to show me, dumb dumb. And it's called a jack and it's what you're supposed to slap your hand on when you see it appear on the pile of cards in between us. Now again, like I showed you before." I put a card down and then he slowly followed suit and then we repeated until a jack appeared on the pile and I slapped my hand down making him jump.

I earned the pile of cards in the middle of us and collected them from my victory. Earlier, he had asked if we could play a game, something from this day and age and the only thing I had in my bag was a pack of cards and the only game besides *'go fish'* was *'slap-jack'* and that's what we were currently playing.

Seeing him look at each card like it was a strange animal in his hands, was entertaining enough for me. I reached back and flipped my long hair out of the way and let it rest on my back. I loved the new color and thought about keeping it permanently. I wondered what my sister would think about the color choice.

Thinking about my sister made me sad but looking up and seeing his little bit of happiness by just holding and learning a new game would be enough of a distraction for myself. Missing her would have to come later, and I knew that she could fend for herself and I knew that she would heal from the wound he gave her. I also thought about Margaret and her little secret she told me that night. If she had been there when he was cursed, then maybe she could help us. "Cyrus, what do you think about bringing someone to the castle to help us do something?" His eyes left the cards in his hands and looked at me.

He stopped looking at me and let his eyes wander around the room. He sat up straighter and got more comfortable on the bed we had been sitting on. I hoped my question wasn't going to make him uncomfortable. "Who will it be and for what reason?" His words were small and soft as he watched his cards and waited for my response. "Her name is Margaret, she owns the bookstore in the town. She told me a while ago that she is a… That she's… Um…" I was hesitating, I wasn't sure how he would deal with the fact that I knew a witch. "What is the matter? Is she weird or something?" He looked back to his cards and I tried to get up the nerve to tell him. "She's a witch, and before you say something-" But I didn't get the chance to explain myself because in a flash, he was off the bed and pacing the room. "How could you even ask me that question? You know that a damn witch did this to me! Why would you even think that I would allow another inside these walls?" He was mad and that was obvious, I didn't want to make him mad, but I wanted to know if Margaret could help us at all. I just needed to explain to him that she was a good witch. "Cyrus hear me out, she's not like the one that cursed you!" I was trying to plead my case, but I knew he wasn't going to listen. I would have to make him. "They are all the same, Henrietta! Spineless, cruel, and a waste of a human life. They may seem nice and good at first, but they will turn on you just like that witch turned on my father." His face should have been red with anger, instead it was pale with a gray sheen like usual. "This one is good, I swear! I've known her since we moved here and she's a good person, I don't even think she practices magic much anymore. The only reason I thought she would be good for our situation because she was there, before you were cursed. She may know the witch and maybe we could get this lifted, through her powers."

I jumped off the bed and stood in front of his fuming body. He was nearly shaking with rage and I hoped that I wasn't going to push him off the edge. "So instead of getting absolutely mad with any sort of idea about having a witch in the castle again, maybe you can sit and listen to what she may or may not have to say." He looked at the ground and then at me again, almost seeming like he was going to calm down but when his eyes met mine again he turned around quickly and ran out of the room, slamming the door in his wake.

I was tired of him always leaving when he was mad or sad and I wasn't going to have it this time. I ran after him slamming the door just as hard as he had. I followed him and had made it all the way to the front foyer only to see him standing in the middle of the room. I walked up to him cautiously like you would if you wanted to approach a bear. "Cyrus, have you calmed down yet? Can we talk about this?" I used my sweet yet condescending voice to try and get him to talk back to me without biting my head off.

I walked closer and closer to him without him saying a word and as I got closer he stayed the same, staring out the window. There was something wrong and I wasn't sure what it was, but if it's spooking Cyrus then it had to be important. "Cyrus? What's wrong?" I was shoulder to arm with him and looking out at the same place he was which was one of the windows in the stone wall, well, more like a large square hole since they didn't have glass windows then. "Someone is out there… I can smell them, they have been here for a while. Maybe a week." That freaked me out right then and there. No one was supposed to know about what was going on in this castle, as far as anyone down there was concerned, this was an abandoned castle. "Who do you think it is?" I asked him to know he most likely didn't know. "Not sure, I have been out of the loop for some time now and I do not know anyone but you from the town below me. Let us find out, shall we?" He looked down at me and smiled, obviously forgetting our discussion from earlier.

He walked over to the window as I followed behind him. The sun wasn't on this side of the castle at the moment, so his hand would be safe from the glaring sun's rays. I stood behind him when he reached out and suddenly grabbed something. His face contorted a bit and then lifted something from the ground below the window, or more like someone. When he brought the little spy into the house through the window, I couldn't believe who it was. Cyrus brought the spy and sat them on the ground inside the castle. When I got a full look at him, I nearly punched him in the face myself. "What the hell are you doing here, Gregory?" His face went from mine to Cyrus' and then the screaming started.

Gregory Rice

What the hell was Gregory Rice doing spying on the castle? With all of his advances and his horrible flirting, did he really graduate to stalking?

Maybe, he saw me go into it the last time he saw me? Whatever the reason was it was going to stop, he didn't need to be sticking his nose in where it didn't belong. And whatever this was or is, was definitely not his business.

His screaming hadn't stopped, and it was beginning to annoy us both. I looked over at Cyrus who was rubbing his temples either trying to ease the headache that was sure to be forming or trying to hold himself back from killing the screamer. "I don't think he's going to stop anytime soon, should we just tie him to a chair or something?" I suggested to him to make the screaming stop. "Sounds good, get the big one out of the dining room. Please." I stopped walking towards the dining room when I heard the *please* from him, it was little things like that that made me think he was going to be okay... Eventually.

I got to the dining room and found the closest chair to the door. Remembering that these chairs were sturdy and very heavy, the only way I was going to get it out of here was to drag it like a dead body.

The chair itself was taller than me and that's saying something because I was not that short. The weight of the chair dug into my hands as I dragged it to the front foyer. I thought about how we were going to keep his mouth shut when we didn't have any tape to shut it physically, we may have to just talk him into not screaming any more.

I dragged the chair until I got back to the foyer where Cyrus was still standing in front of the now sobbing ball of what used to be Gregory Rice. I rolled my eyes and put the chair next to the sobbing man-boy. Making sure the chair was on all four feet, I went back to standing next to Cyrus. "When did he finally stop screaming?" I asked Cyrus while watching him stare at the two of us. "Not long after you left, and I do believe it is because of the way I look. I did not think I was that scary looking." I looked at him and saw the same face I always did and could not see a reason to be scared of it. I think I saw a bit of pride in his eyes, but I think that was covering up the shame I knew he felt in his appearance.

I decided that it was my duty to get the reason why he was really here out of him. He was most likely following me as per usual.

Cyrus walked over to him and bent down to lift his slumped-over body into the air so that he could tie him to the chair. I looked around the room to try and find something to tie him up with and a possible gag.

Not thinking I was going to find anything, I actually came across some old phone wire in the bag that Cyrus had brought up along with the cry baby Gregory. I also dug around a bit more and found a large stash of junk food. He was right, he had to have been staying out there for a week or two. And the more I thought about that, the more I realized if he hadn't been leaving and coming back then he was going to the bathroom out there. Gross.

I tossed the phone cord to Cyrus and after he looked it over for about five minutes, he tied the still crying Gregory to the chair and I brought over an old sock I found in his bag. Not wanting to hear the crying any more, I shoved the sock into his mouth and watched his tear-filled eyes go wide when he saw me stuff the nasty sock into his mouth.

I was glad he was shocked, he needed to realize the world wasn't his to just snoop around on. He was so nosy. "Okay Gregory, I will ask you this once and I'll take the sock out of your mouth. Why were you out there spying on us?" I reached down and took the sock from his mouth. I stood back when he began to spit trying to get the yuck out of his mouth from the sock. "What the hell Henrietta! You can't just tie me up and gag me with a sock! What's wrong with you?" I rolled my eyes and shoved the sock back into his mouth. "That was not the answer to my question. Now, to get the gag out of your mouth, you must answer my question. Can you do that for me?" I was leaning on my knees with my eyes down to his level, waiting for the nod that told me he understood what I was talking about. "If I may say something." Cyrus spoke up behind me. I turned around and listened to what he wanted to say. "Seeing as you know this boy, I will let you go ahead with the torture, you seem to be doing a great job as it is anyways." His smile showed a bit of pride towards how I was handling things and honestly it made me beam. "Now, are you going to answer my question?" He nodded his head yes and I took the smelly sock out of his mouth again. "I started after that night you ran me over with the scooter, the next day I decided to follow you to where you had been hiding at instead of going to school. When I saw that you were cleaning I was just going to leave but then I saw that... that thing with you. You were laughing and teaching him things, like he's a lost puppy or something. I find it disgusting." He spit towards Cyrus and I lost it.

I threw a hard-right hand punch to his face and nearly knocked him and the chair onto the ground. When his face came back into my view, I threw my left fist into his face again and knocked him the other way. "You don't have the right to call him disgusting, you low life. You are the one stalking me and practically have been since I was fourteen years old, you are the sick one. Pay him some respect, you bastard. I'm going to let you go without another punch, but you better swear on your life that you will never come back. And if you break that promise, I will personally beat the ever lovin' shit out of you." I was an inch away from his face and watching the sweat roll down his forehead. "You wouldn't dare lay another hand on me if you know what's good for you." I was about to rebuttal his award-winning argument but I was pulled backwards before I could.

In my place, Cyrus stood and bent down to his level with his hands behind his back. Obviously upset at the threat he just spewed at me because he grabbed Gregory by his shirt and brought him up to his standing level, chair and all. A low growl came from Cyrus and the more that I thought about it, the more I knew that I didn't want to see his face right now. Especially his eyes. I had no doubt that they were pitch black. "You dare threaten her in my presence! I am the wrong person to say that in front of, because I WILL rip your head off and wave it like a flag over your limp body. And if I ever see you again, you will not be walking away like she will reluctantly do, because she is a good person." He threw him down and let the chair catch his fall, then he stormed off and waited for me to take out the rest of the trash.

I walked up to him and untied the restraints and brought him to his feet by right ear. Walking him to the main door, I opened the door and pushed him out the rest of the way. "Leave here and never return." With my parting words, I slammed the heavy door in his shocked and bruised face.

No one threatened Cyrus, not without my permission. No one.

What Sort of Witch?

"I do not like this idea at all." I knew he wouldn't, we had been discussing it for about five minutes and that's all he had to say. He didn't like it.

I knew he didn't like it, he'd made that painfully clear, but it needed to happen, I had a good feeling about this. Like the fact that it really needed to happen, he needed to fill in the blanks of things he missed or didn't know, like his father not really wanting all of this and was double crossed by the witch.

But this was a different witch! It had to be different; she just had to be.

I dug out the phone I never used and brought into the light of the room. Before I started to power it up, I saw a shadow cross over me. Looking up, I saw Cyrus' curious eyes looking over the smart phone in my hands. He didn't even look at me, his eyes were glued to the phone. "Would you like to see what it actually does? Or is staring at it good enough for you?" I looked up at him and watched his eyes detach from the phone and land on me. "If you do not mind, yes, I would like to see whatever that is. Also, that boy Grape or whatever you called him, left his bag and there are strange noises coming from it." I handed him the phone and walked to the bag that Gregory left here.

I started rummaging through the bag and came across the same junk food from before. My stomach began to growl, and I did the most logical thing, I ripped open a bag of chips and began munching on them. Gregory would call then crisps and tell me how even after five years of living here I still didn't act like I belonged here, and he was right, I didn't belong here. He always made fun of me for being from America.

After searching through the rest of the bag, I found nothing make any sound even his phone was turned off. Now that I thought about it, he was most likely hearing the sound of the phone dying. Shaking my head, I stood up from the bag and turned to the ever so curious Cyrus and the smart phone. He stopped looking at the phone and looked at what was in my hand. I usually didn't like eating in my room but since we brought everything up here, I may as well.

I moved the bag around in my hand and he followed it with his eyes like a kitten. "Do you want to try some? I wasn't sure if you could eat regular food or not." I shoved the bag towards him and he took a step back. "They are potato chips. They cut potatoes very thin and then fry them in oil and then season them with different flavorings. And *voilà*, potato chips. Try one, if it makes you sick you know where the bathroom is." He looked at me and then at the chips, it was a wonder he had done anything before he was cursed.

He slipped his hand into the bag and brought out a chip, throwing it into his mouth he crunched down on it, the flavor must have hit his tongue because he smiled, and a brightness shot into his eyes. I couldn't imagine if I had given him anything other than sour cream and onion. Maybe salt and vinegar flavored should wait until he was used to them. "Anyways, give me my phone back, you can have the chips, and I'm calling Margaret to come here. Your petty reasons are being put aside for now." I didn't really think he was listening to me because all I heard was crunching and a bit of mumbling, but no back talk.

I searched through my phone and quickly responded to the messages my sister left for me. I told her that I was okay and that she shouldn't worry. Of course, that wasn't going to stop her for doing so, but at least I knew she was safe.

I found Margaret's number and gave her a ring. After a few rings on the other line she answered with her usual greeting. "Bookworm Bookstore, we have all your favorites guaranteed." I smiled at the greeting and prepared myself to speak with a known witch. "Hey Margaret, its Henrietta." I waited for her to freak out and then came back down to earth to speak with me. That was why I didn't call her very often. "Wow! Henrietta, I didn't think I would be hearing from you, at least not over the phone or anything. I went to go see your sister yesterday and she told me a wild story. But that we can talk about later. Sooo, what's going on? Need a book?" She was chipper and didn't seem like she cared at all about what I told her over a month ago. "No, actually I need a delivery, but not for books. I need you to come to the castle and speak with the prince. He's not too up for it but I think his mind will change once he meets you. Please?" I put everything I had into the word please and with that I knew she would cave. "I would love to come and meet him, just give me like twenty minutes and I'll be there." She hung up the phone without another word and I clicked my end off as well.

Looking up at him with his face inside the bag of chips, I lost my shit. I started laughing which made him jump.

I laughed so hard that I started choking on my own spit. Turning a laughing fit into a coughing fit, I sat down on the edge of the bed while Cyrus put the bag down and walked over to me. He bent down and pulled my chin to his, his face was filled with worry and I hadn't seen that in him before. "Are you alright?" His worry made me start laughing again, just less violently. "Yes, I'm fine, you just made me laugh a little too hard and then I started coughing. I just need to take a breather, its fine. Thanks for the concern." I gently pushed his hand away from my face and watched as he stood back up.

I grabbed the now empty bag of chips and threw them in a trash bag. "Margaret is on her way. You're going to play nice and find out what she knows about everything. Okay? If you can't do it for her since she's a witch, just do it for yourself. Do it for the fact that she may have information on the curse." I nodded my head and didn't take any lip back from him. "I realize I cannot change your mind on this but how do we know which witch she is?" His question confused me a bit. "What do you mean?" I asked him back. "Which witch will she be, or more like what kind of witch is she? Will she turn on us like the one who is responsible for this whole mess, or will she actually help me?" Now I was getting it, he was scared that she would double cross us like the other witch. "I'll make sure she doesn't, okay? If I even think she is going to do something that would put any of our progress in jeopardy, then I would get rid of her. Period. No questions asked." I gave him a mock salute and headed out of the room to go wait for her to arrive.

This would be a good thing, I just knew it. She wasn't going to double cross us and I believed that she would do more good than Cyrus thought. She just had to. And if I believed hard enough, maybe this nagging feeling in my stomach would go away.

A Witch Named Decebal

Cyrus

A knock sounded at the front door to the castle and neither of us moved to open the door. I felt better knowing I was not the only one worried about what this friend of hers may say about the situation.

I was nervous to say the least, I did not want a witch in this castle ever again, but if this plan was going to work then Henrietta needed to trust me and I needed to trust her. I stopped trusting a lot of people after my mother took her own life, the one person in the world that I trusted without question. Then I turned to my father and tried to trust him, but he shut me out and after that, I decided I wasn't worthy of anyone's trust and no one was worthy of mine.

I wanted to blame everything on him, but I knew that was not the right thing to do. I got myself into this mess and I will get myself out.

I looked down at Henrietta and nudged her a bit to answer the door. She seemed to be daydreaming because she had to shake her head before she walked towards the door. Maybe she was putting too much stock into this witch helping us.

I stood up straight and waited for the door to open, revealing the witch behind it. Maybe I was a little biased, but I just did not like witches, not any more.

She let the door swing open and then the witch walked into the foyer with the both of us. I could tell from here that she was much older than she seemed. Witches were tricky and one of their tricks was their age. They looked young until they hit a certain age then it was like watching a fruit go bad. They would quickly age and be near death within a few years of hitting the aging mark. "Margaret, thank you for coming. This is Prince Cyrus, I'm sure you already know him." She introduced me to

Margaret and I did not know why she thought she would know me. Now that I looked at her, she did seem familiar, a young beauty if you will, just not my type. Witch or not. "Let's just go sit in the kitchen and get this awkward situation underway, shall we?" Henrietta moved us all to the kitchen, nearly forcing me after the witch through the doorway.

I dragged my feet and stood on the opposite side of wherever the witch stood. I could smell the magic on her and I hated it. I hated magic.

I did, however, like that I could smell something other than the putrid rot I was used to, from being created out of magic for so long, I used to hate the heightened senses that the curse gave me because I was trapped in that room, but now I could open them up more. I was not smelling just magic and my decaying body. "Okay, let's just get down to why you're here, Margaret. I know you're a witch because you told me, he knows you're a witch because I told him, and because he can smell it on you." She turned and looked at me. How did she know that? "It's because you make this face when you smell something odd." She answered my silent question. If she kept that up, I would not need to speak in this conversation. "You told me yourself that you were alive when he was human, before he was cursed. Can you tell us anything about the witch that did the curse or the curse itself? Maybe even how to break it." She sounded like she was near begging, and here I thought she was not that invested in our situation.

Perhaps, I was more convincing than I thought. Getting the curse breaker to figure this all out was a lot easier than I imagined, the hard part was the other half of me wanting something more when it was all said and done. That was the part I was trying to suffocate at the moment and pretend that it did not exist to begin with. "I would need to know more about what really happened. Back then, I wasn't a part of any covens or anything. I was just starting out, a preteen I believe. I think I was around ten or twelve when the queen had passed away and maybe my early twenties, by looks alone, when you had been cursed. I practiced some, but I didn't really get into it until after my first hundred years." I watched the witch shrug and fiddle with the ring on her finger; she was hiding something. "Okay, Cyrus could you tell us the story? If you can that is." She was sweet to take my feelings into consideration, but I could do this. I just hoped I would not look different to her after she heard the truth. "Of course, I can tell you what really happened between the witch and me leading her to curse me.

"It was the year 1701 and I was around ten, almost eleven years old. It had been nearly six years since my mother had passed along with my sister and I had not gotten any better. My father had turned cold and cruel towards me as his son, rarely ever speaking more than a word in my direction. I had decided to go fishing one day and I knew there was a stream with some fish in it behind the castle and down the road.

I had to sneak out of the castle so that a guard or a nanny did not follow me. I had a pole and some string in my arms and a bucket for anything I would catch that day.

I headed out of the castle and made my way down to the small creek, I sat up all my things and started my day of fishing. This was one of the last days before the curse that I was ever well-behaved. I was not sure on the amount of time that had passed before a small boy had come up to me.

This boy was probably a few years older than I was and I had never seen him before around the kingdom, which did not say much since I rarely left without an escort. Regardless, the boy tried to steal my fishing pole and what I had caught that day, that is when things went sour.

I was mad enough that I was being neglected by my father and that my mother left me, which I had blamed myself for, and now this little boy was stealing my things. When I pulled the fishing pole out of his grasp, he tripped over the bucket in front of him and fell face first into the creek. He would have been fine if I had just walked away but a hatred fell over me and it was something I did not feel in control of and I had decided that his life was worth less than mine.

I walked up to the boy that was trying to get out of the creek and instead of helping him out of the water, I sat on his back and held his head under the stream. I stayed on his back until he stopped moving.

As I got up to leave, I saw a woman with bright red hair standing on the hill by the creek. She had tears in her eyes and an underlying hatred that was pointed towards me. Her stare

128

burned a hole through my body. I walked past her and as I did, she screamed the boy's name and ran to him. As I was leaving for the castle as if nothing had gone on, she screamed towards me that she would have her revenge.

When she cursed me that night and I opened my eyes to see her dangling a dagger over my chest, I saw the bright red hair and the tears that seemed to still fall from her eyes. I knew right then that I had made a terrible mistake. I never figured she would hold a grudge against me for nearly nine years. She must have waited for her chance and then took it when my father was desperate for help."

I finished with my story and looked around at the eyes in the room. Henrietta was looking at her fingers and then back at me. It was a look that I never wanted her to have towards me, a look of shame.

I looked at the witch and she held the same reflective tears in her eyes. "The only witch I knew back then with the red hair you spoke about would be a witch named Decebal. You killed her son that day. Decebal was also known as one of the more powerful practicing witches of her time but to me, she was only known by one name. Mother." The witch looked me dead in the eyes and I saw Henrietta shift next to her. "Does that mean that the little boy was-" She was cut off by the witch in front of me. "Yes, my brother, he killed my brother." The witch did not waste another word, instead she lunged for my throat.

One Side or the Other

Henrietta

I watched as Margaret lunged for Cyrus' throat, usually being quick to think and to take action, I snapped out of my daydream and I lunged at Margaret and did the only thing I could. I grabbed a fist full of her light hair and yanked her back before she could make contact with Cyrus.

I wasn't happy about what he told her either and I understood her pain and her want to hurt him, but I still wasn't going to let her.

I pulled her back to the stool she had been perched on before and I didn't let go until she stopped trying to get back up. She was strong, and I knew that I wouldn't be able to hold her for much longer. I needed him to leave the room. "Cyrus, go to my room and we will discuss this later. Now." I wasn't leaving him room to argue about what I was telling him to do. It was for his own safety.

He gave me a look like he wasn't going to do what I told him, but when I yanked her hair back again, he finally got the message and left the room. She finally stopped thrashing around when he left, and I decided that now was a good time to stop pulling on her hair. "What the hell Margaret, I bring you here and you attack him. I know the story must have hit you hard, but you have a mouth, you should have used that first." I threw my hands in the air and looked at her for a response. "I was trying to use my mouth, but he wasn't close enough, then someone pulled my god damn hair!" If I wasn't so mad at her right now, I would have laughed but now was not the time. "I understand your pain, I understand why you tried to injure him, but I don't want violence right now, it's not the time. We need answers about that curse and we need them now. Since the

130

curse giver was your mother, you must know something about it!" I was yelling now, and I didn't really want to calm down. She needed to know I meant business. "You think I would help you now? Now that I know he was the one that killed my little brother. I understand now why my mother never told me who it was, she was working on her own plan for revenge. Well, I'm not going to interrupt her little plan. You'll pry that knowledge out of my cold dead hands."

I slammed my fist on the counter top and made her head turn back to me. "That scenario can be arranged, I can bring you to the brink of death with only one thought left in your mind, *'I should have told her the answer before she tried to cut my throat.'* And I will not regret doing it. Because you see I know, that you know, that I am connect to this whole thing. And I would very much like to know why you were the one that started all of it." Her eyes met mine and I could have sworn I saw regret behind them, but I wasn't certain. "What do you mean? I didn't tell you to go to the castle and set free a possible tyrant." I gave her a confused look, he wasn't a tyrant. "No, you wouldn't know that, would you? If he had taken the throne, he wouldn't have been a king, he would have turned into a tyrant. A mad king. That is the reason why his father called upon my mother for her help. My mother's plan was set into motion after that." I shook my head, things weren't making much sense. "His father wasn't going to give him the crown because of his behavior, now unless he started turning things around, the king had already planned to teach him a lesson. Why would he have turned into a tyrant?" I needed answers while she was still here. "Don't you get it, Henri? My mother's plan was put into action long before she cursed him. After the day my brother was killed, she swore on his grave that she would make the person who did it pay. She would drive them insane with her magic, to the point that their inner colors and desires came through to the surface. She explained it to me like this, the day she watched my brother's killer walk past her she saw the regret and the guilt in his eyes, but she didn't want him to feel that. She wanted him to suffer."

Okay, this was going on a tangent a bit and she needed to reel this story in. "What I mean is if my mother hadn't gone after his mind like she did, the prince would have turned his life around, that was the moment he was supposed to see what a horrible person he had become. That was the day he was supposed to change and better himself. Instead, she made him think about that day along with his mother's death until he went mad. He sentenced people to death left and right for the tiniest things or for nothing at all. She drove him to become the monster he was and then she got herself hired to curse him and of course, you know the story about that."

She was right, I did, she double crossed the king and put an actual curse on him instead of just scaring him. "That's right, she double crossed the king. She came home that day and told me to write the book I traded you. She told me to write a fairy tale that someday would make someone think that the prince was real and could be cured. The day your sister and you crossed that border was the same day I stumbled upon the book again. I hadn't seen or touched it in three hundred years, but that day it chose to come out. For you. I knew that you would be the sucker to think they could break the curse. That you were the miraculous knight that would save the prince. But when I heard you let him out, I knew the final part of my mother's plan was going to happen instead."

Her twisted smile and deep laugh nearly made me shake with fear. I had never, ever, seen her like this, but then again, I was a fool for believing anything she had to say. This was my mistake and I needed to make things right. "What is the final part of her plan?" I asked hoping it was something I could prevent. "Her final piece of the plan was that if he was ever released from his prison cell, that he would kill the entire town and the knight that brought him back. She hates this town and to see the last of the people from the ones that lived in it so long ago burn with their houses and their pride, she would be so happy." I almost bought into what she was saying but right when she spoke about her mother hating the town below, I found my loophole. "You said she hates the town, not hated. She's still alive, isn't she?" With the realization of what I had just figured out plastered across her face, I smiled. I had found my loophole and a very real way of breaking this curse. "Whose side are you really on, Henri? The prince that killed hundreds or the people that tried to stop him?" Her words were like ice in the air, chilling everything around them. "This isn't some game of red rover where I have to pick a side to join. I'm on the side of freeing a man that has paid for his crimes long enough. A man that is truly sorry for what he did, and that includes your brother. A man that I believe is good, down to the soul he thinks he's lost. Maybe I should be asking you whose side you're on."

And with my last word, Cyrus came through the entrance of the kitchen, picked her up off the stool, and carried her to the front door. I followed after them and watched as he opened the door and threw her to the front yard. "We have work to do." I spoke to him as he let the door shut behind him.

Summoning a Plan

I was furious to say the least, this whole experience was practically set up for us and it pissed me off. I stormed through the castle and made it to the room where all my crap was hiding and searched for the one thing I assumed would give us a sliver of hope. I riffled through my stuff and through the random junk that was in the room. I was supposed to be the tidy one and here I stood in the middle of a massive mess. I didn't even think I had brought this much stuff, but my go bag had more in it then I remembered.

When my fingers finally met what I was looking for, I snatched it up off the ground. Forgetting the weight that it had, I nearly dropped it when I picked it up.

From the corner of my eye, I saw Cyrus enter the room with more slump than usual. I turned to him with the book he made himself and I mean literally made himself, of himself, and swung my head towards the bed to signal to him to follow me.

I watched him do so and as I got comfortable on the bed and saw him crawl onto the bed and sit as I was sitting. I put the large book in the middle of us and began turning the thick pages looking for something I could use. "She's alive, the witch that cursed you and turned you mad, she's alive and I have a plan to kill her." I didn't bother looking up at him because I knew his face would hold shock. But like I had said, I was pissed. "How do you propose we do that? Just summon her here and stick a knife in her heart and hope for the best?" I looked up to see a smug almost snide look on his face. "No, I don't think that would work, summoning doesn't work. It's just a thing you see in movies." I shrugged my shoulders as I tried to tell him off. "What is a movie? And summoning is a real thing, we would just need a spell book which would not be in this place. And, of course, ingredients that the summoning would call for. Which could be hard to find." He spoke as if he was far off, perhaps thinking about an actual summons. I didn't know if I could wrap my head around doing an actual summons. But I would give it a try if it meant taking that bitch down for good. "We can get back to the movie thing, but first where would we get a spell book?" I thought about for a second and before I let Cyrus answer, I smacked myself in the face for not realizing it before. "Oh my god, Margaret's store, of course. She owns a bookstore and she's a witch, she has got to have a spell book or two in there." I was currently standing on the bed jumping around happy that I found a possible way on hunting down that witch. "Earlier, I had only caught a bit of what the other witch was telling you, but I did not hear everything, could you tell me the rest. Mainly about how the witch made me go mad?" His eyes fell to his hands and it was like I could feel the weight of the guilt that it had been his fault the entire time just come off him.

I was happy that it wasn't all him, I was still pissed as hell that the witch did all of this to him making him believe that he was such a bad person, letting him deal with all of this by himself, even letting him live with the guilt of killing people. I hated her.

I sat back down on the bed and stopped my jumping. I prepared myself for telling him the awful truth or at least the rest of it. "She told me that her mother, Decebal, the one that cursed you started on the curse way before that night she *killed* you. She said the day that she saw you kill her son you showed a face of regret and guilt, and that made her really angry and she wanted you to suffer. She put a spell on you so that you wouldn't feel guilt basically, you wouldn't regret your actions, and hopefully you would leave the town barren like she really wanted. She was a twisted person." I spoke to him calmly and with as much information as I could. "So that day, I really did feel guilt for killing that boy? I thought this whole time that I was a monster for not feeling anything when he died. I should have changed my ways if I had felt the guilt of that first kill, but she blocked it all from me. She is the reason I sentenced people to death without a second thought. I did things without thinking. I could have been a great king and person if she would have just let me be. She should have let me live with the guilt and let that turn me into a better person." He was mad now and I could see it in his eyes; he wanted blood. "I read more about the curse she laid on you. It's meant to allow you to live for eternity with your outside matching your inside and at that moment your inside was falling apart and was nearing a death like state, so that is what you can blame for your outside looking like it does. The whole drinking blood thing like a vampire and having the fangs is a part of the survival trait she gave you, you have to suck the life force from other beings like a leech in order to survive without agonizing pain." I read from the book Margaret had given me and looked up some things in the other book he made. "That would explain why I had less pain when I fed off you and your sister. Since then, the pain has come back but it is something I can handle, you need not worry yourself." I smiled at him because he picked up on my worried face, we had been getting closer these last few weeks. I just hope that he didn't retreat into himself again, it felt like we had to start over when he did that. "Now, the curse says that you need someone else to break it for you, but Margaret said her mother made it to where you could never find that person. Then why was I sent here? I thought you said I was supposed to help break it?" His eyes shifted around the room and finally landed back on me. "I tore out the part that involves you. The part that I tore said that someone will come along that is the curse's equal yet opposite." I squinted at him with my brain going to different ways. "What does that mean?" I asked him after trying to figure it out. "It means that I am someone that has done great negative things and the opposite would be someone that great negative things have happened to them, or that they have done great positive things. And that is you, you have had terrible things happen to you in your past, but you haven't done anything negative and I have done terrible things in my past to other people. We are supposed to balance each other out and be able to figure out the cure. But if the witch put some sort of cause on it that is supposed to drive me insane, enough to kill everyone down in the town and you, then I am out of ideas."

He threw his hands in the air and let them fall back down to his lap. I didn't have much of an idea either, but I still thought summoning that witch might be a start. "Let's go get that book." His eyes met mine and he gave me a mischievous smile. It was time I showed off my odd talent at breaking and entering.

Talent Show

"Okay, so we now know that a black spaghetti strap shirt does not go with your body type, let's try this." I held up a plain black shirt to his chest and gave it a look. "This looks better, try this shirt on." He reluctantly took the shirt from my hands and walked to the bathroom.

We were currently getting ready to break into the bookworm bookstore that I used to frequent. We needed a spell book and although the store wasn't a witchcraft store, the owner was a witch and it was our best bet to find one.

But to do this we needed the right clothes which was why I was trying to get Cyrus dressed in all black clothing instead of whatever the hell he was wearing the day he was imprisoned. Now that I thought about it, he wasn't used to wearing something that was so thin like a regular t-shirt. Which made it all the more hilarious when I put him in a tank top with little to no straps.

He kept covering his arms like it was such a horrible thing to have exposed arms. I guess it makes sense since he was wearing like two layers of long sleeves before I asked him to strip them off and put on what I had in my bag. Which I had to hand wash after he decided to take a bath that day.

When he walked out of the bathroom in one of my old black t-shirts that I used when I didn't want to put on pants to go to sleep, yeah, I was letting him wear an old jammie shirt. It was the only thing I had that was long enough to actually go down to his waist, the long giant. "I do not think this is appropriate, just a shirt and some, what did you call theses?" He pulled at the fabric that covered his legs and I laughed a little. I can't believe he let me put a pair of black sweatpants on him. "They are sweatpants, cotton or polyester blend and they are used for when you want to feel comfortable. Do you not like them?" I asked as he kept looking at the fabric covering his legs and waist. "It is just a strange feeling. So little clothes and so much softer than what I am used to. It is surprising that your clothes fit me." He stopped looking at what he was wearing and then at me. "Yeah, well I always own a few shirts and pants that are way too big for me. Plus, since you've been imprisoned, you must have lost a lot of weight and you still aren't up to your healthy pounds yet." I looked at him in hopes that I hadn't offended him in any way. "That is true although the before time, I was not very large either. My father was a large man, tall and all muscle, my mother was small but tall as well. There was not much to lose in that cell, but I am wanting to get back to my original weight. Less bone more meat so to speak." He pulled at the black shirt and walked around trying to find something. "What are you looking for?" I asked him as he started to riffle through things. "Shoes. I was hoping when they shut the castle down they left a few of my things, but since I cannot find anything of mine in my old room, I need shoes." He kept looking through things and I thought about what I had brought there and I didn't remember if I had other shoes here. "Well, you may have to go without because I don't even think I have shoes for myself. There aren't any rocks or anything on the way there, it's all concrete so I think we'll be okay." I shrugged my shoulders and watched him go and sit on the bed waiting for me.

I walked around the room filling one of my bags with the rest of the things I might need to break into the bookstore. When I had finally finished, I stood in front of the bed and waited for him to notice that I was ready and waiting on him. "What's up buttercup?" I nonchalantly said to him, as I started for the front door. "What? What is buttercup?" He asked me in an almost broken English accent, sometimes I forgot that he didn't always understand what I was saying. And since I'd lived in this country for five years, the accent thing had kind of gotten old so when he talked like that his accent got deeper and just a bit different than what I was used to.

Smiling at him, I shook my head and tried not to laugh at him. "It's just a saying, I'll explain that to you later." I waved a hand and walked out the front door, before he followed me out however, I grabbed the stone that was wedged in between two others on the wall by the door of the castle. Walking back to the door, I handed the stone to him and he walked out without a scratch on him. One of the more annoying things about the curse, I should just crush it up and put it in a vial or something small like that.

The stone thing often confused me because if the witch wanted him to go crazy and destroy everything and everyone, why would she bind him to the castle? Maybe she was hoping he would find the loophole, and the time he was bound to the castle he would have gone insane enough for him to destroy everything.

Something I will have to figure out later.

We started off down the hill of the castle and surprisingly, there were no stickers or thorns in the grass. We made it all the way to the sidewalk before Cyrus spoke up about something. "How are we going to get in there if it is locked?" I stopped walking to actually look at him in surprise. "You do know that we are going to break into the store, right? You realize if Margaret was there at this time of night or even if we had gone during store hours, she wouldn't have just let us in. That's why we are going after store hours and at night, that way we won't get caught and we can just go in and out, and there would be no problem." We started walking again in silence and nearly got all the way there before he asked another question. "So how are you going to get in?" He was so innocent, at least to these times. "I have a special talent that allows me to get into buildings that are locked. Don't worry, you'll see." I walked in front of him leading the way.

It didn't take long to get to the bookstore and when we did, I dug through my bag to find the two things I would need to pick the lock. Bringing out the two small metal picks from my bag, I looked both ways and started on the metal knob in my hands. "Cy, don't let anyone see what we're doing, okay?" He gave me a weird look when he heard the nickname I gave him but still did as I asked.

Piercing the lock hole with the metal picks and turning them in just the right way, I earned a click and turn from the door knob. I looked up at Cyrus, who was looking at the unlocked door with amazement in his eyes. "Neat talent, huh?" I spoke to him before opening the door to the bookstore. I paused before opening the door more just in case she had anything set up for an alarm or something. After not hearing anything for a couple of minutes, I opened the door all the way and walked inside. "Are you certain that we are safe in here? No one will come in on us while we are looking for the book?" He asked in a whispered tone, even leaning down towards my ear more. "I'm not one hundred percent sure but if we hurry and stop asking questions we could be out of here in a few minutes. So, let's go." I hurried him along and headed for where I knew she kept the more important books that no one in this town could even thought about buying because they were too expensive and until now, I never knew why she had them, but I realize now that she was hiding her little secret in plain sight.

Hurrying to the shelf I needed, I ran my finger down each spine until I found what we needed. *Everything you need to know about summoning*. I looked it over and thought who the hell would name a book that? It's like it's a book for dummies. *'Summoning for dummies'* I thought to myself and then snickered at the actual book and its title and then turned to Cyrus. "Okay, got it, let's go." He turned around and headed for the door like I had.

We got back to the front door and as I went to close the door and lock it back, a thought entered my head. I had been thinking how easy this all was, how nothing went wrong for once and I knew I shouldn't have been thinking that because that would be an automatic jinx. If I believed in that sort of thing.

We both turned and started down the street and when I turned the corner to start for the castle, I ran into the last person I wanted to see.

The Chase

"Why is it that every time I turn a corner or I look out a window, even walking down the sidewalk, it's you? I get no rest from your god forsaken face!" I screamed at the person we just happened to run into when we turned the corner.

And of course, it was Gregory Rice, the one person I seemed to never be able to get rid of. I rolled my eyes when his met mine and then moved over to see Cyrus standing behind me. I heard a low growl come from behind my back and I knew I needed to get him out of here because I wasn't going to try and predict what he was going to do. "Well, this was not fun, but we have somewhere else we want to be." I pushed past Gregory and honestly it was getting real old running into him all the time, it was like he knew where I would be all the time and that was one thing that did scare me. Guy with fangs not so much, but a guy that knew my every move, yeah it wigged me out.

When we got a few feet away from Gregory, I heard him shout something I didn't quite catch.

I turned around to look at what he wanted, so that he didn't follow us back to the castle. But what I saw surprised me. There Gregory was, standing with what I could only figure was a very sharp knife in his hand.

Seeing this nearly didn't register in my head because it was so ridiculous looking. Gregory with a knife! How absurd. When he started coming towards us with the knife, I didn't back away because it was *Gregory Rice* with a *knife*, it was like a puppy acting like a big dog. But when I saw someone come from around the corner with a knife that looked strikingly similar to Gregory's, I started to get a bit tense.

I didn't wait for the other three people that started coming from the same way Gregory and his partner with the knife because I didn't want more attention drawn to Cyrus and me. Plus, that was a lot of knifes and I didn't want to deal with it. "Cy, we need to leave, now. Usually, if it was just one or two I would say we could take them but I'm seeing a fifth person come from behind that corner and we just need to go." He was still standing behind me and when I backed up to start leaving the people with knives coming from the corner, I ran into a wall. A wall named Cyrus. "We cannot just leave them here thinking we are cowards. I can take them, they only have knives. I have fought knights with swords bigger and longer than both of my arms, I can take down a dozen people with knives that are no bigger than my foot." I knew he would say something like this. Crap. I needed him to get out of here, the more exposure he had around town the more people would wonder why a prince that was born in 1690 was still around today. "No! we need to leave, I have no doubt in my mind that you could take all of those people down but right now, we need to keep you safe and under the radar, especially since we just stole something from a witch." I stared him in the eyes and made sure he knew I meant business. "We will do this your way. This time." His deep voice was sending a shiver down my spine, I ignored it of course, since I didn't have time to unlock that box of crazy in my head.

I looked back over to Gregory and his small gang that was starting to form around him. They didn't come further than where he was standing and when I looked around to each of their faces, I saw that they were just regular people from around the town. Somehow Gregory had talked them all into attacking us in the middle of the night with knives. And here I thought he wasn't organized. "Gregory, I see you have joined a gang, but we have no intention of joining, so we are going to leave and if you know what's good for you, you won't follow either of us and you'll go home to your families. Father Donald! I know your wife and daughter wouldn't like what you're doing right now." I singled out one of the followers that Gregory had led to us hoping it would bring someone to their senses. "We've been told the truth, young lady, and we are all here because that abomination cannot continue to live in this town. Either he locks himself back up or we kill him. I'm protecting my family, you would do well to think about your sister as well." Him

143

talking about my sister and implying that I didn't care about her, made me madder than anything. "You are all a bunch of middle aged, big headed, sacred cats that are listening to a child. That's right, Gregory, you're a child, because you and the rest of the people following you, don't know anything about what's going on up at that castle or with the person standing by me. Stay out of our business and we'll leave you alone. Deal?" I stared them all down waiting for someone to defy my speech.

Gregory looked at me like he wanted to serve me up to his dog for lunch, it was a new look on him and I have to say it looked silly. I started taking a step back along with Cyrus and watched the people in the mob in front of us, making sure they didn't make a move on us until we were at least a few blocks away. If we got that chance. "He needs to be taken out, Henrietta, you and I both know it. Now, move aside and allow us to do the work for you." He was just asking to get punched, wasn't he? "You know what Gregory, if you really think you have the strength to kill him and me, because I wouldn't let you get away with just killing him, then you'll have to catch us first." At my last word I turned, grabbed Cyrus' hand, and broke into a run.

I looked back for a split second and as I looked around Cyrus' body, I saw that they indeed were chasing us. I made sure the book we stole was securely in my hand before I started running faster. Dragging Cyrus' body with me, I hoped we could get to the castle before they got us, at least there we have a billion rooms to hide in.

The only thought running through my head was 'catch us if you can'.

Grass Stains and Bloody Noses

I hadn't ran this long since I was in middle school, I was completely out of shape. Cyrus really wasn't much better.

We just needed to get to the castle and we would be safe. Pulling Cyrus behind me, we started for the hill with the castle sitting on it. I felt like we had been running for hours when in reality it was probably only ten or twenty minutes.

Whatever the time it was, it still made me pant like a dog. We made it to the top of the hill and just when I let go of Cyrus' hand, I felt the sharp pain of my hair being pulled and the solid ground I was forced down on. The blur of water from my eyes prevented me from seeing who it was, but I pretty much knew who would have done something like this. "Gregory... Pulling hair is a little bit elementary, don't you think?" I shouted above the mumbling from the mob that had apparently caught up to us. I wiped the tears from my eyes from the yank to my hair. It didn't hurt, it just stung and in turn, it made my eyes water. "If it will get your attention and show you that you're a fool Henrietta, a damn fool. If you just let us have the monster, we will leave you alone and you can go back to your normal life. Your straight A's and perfect attendance. You would be normal again." He was at my level this time and after wiping the water from my eyes, I saw that there were five of the men from the mob, holding Cyrus down to the grown. Probably getting grass stains all over my sweatpants.

I didn't need to be thinking about that right now, not when I had a teenager throwing a fit and pulling my hair. He moved to stand over me now that I was completely laying on my back. I took in another breath in replacing the air that got knocked out of my lungs when I was forced to the ground.

Seeing the only vantage point I could find at the moment, I put my free leg to some good use. Bringing my knee up swiftly and nailing him right in the danglers, forcing *him* down to the ground this time. Using his distracted state to get off the ground and get away from Mr. Black and Blue balls, I picked up the knife he dropped to hold his goods and ran over to the guys trying to hold Cyrus down.

I stood there with the five guys trying to kill Cyrus and tried to find a vantage point so that I could try and throw them off of him. I saw Cyrus in the middle but not in any immediate danger, honestly, they were still trying to pin him down. I took the knife in my hand and walked towards the guys that were really in the way. Walking up to the, what was now a dog pile of men and Cyrus, I grabbed the one closest to me by the hair and pulled him to the ground just as Gregory had done to me. I assumed we were fighting dirty at this point.

When the first guy hit the grass covered ground, I picked my foot up and even without having shoes on, I slammed my heel into the side of his head. I wasn't sure if I knocked him out, but I knew he would at least be dizzy for a while.

I turned around and focused on the next four guys. Once the one was off Cyrus, he was able to knock the rest of them off of his arms and legs. Getting to a standing point, he wobbled over to me and gave me a nod. Looked like our only option was to take these fuckers out.

We stood our ground while the rest of the guys came over to us and stood around our bodies. I felt Cyrus shift his position to where his back was facing my back, meaning the other guys must have circled around us completely.

I had the knife in my hand and the weight of it was making my hand numb, it wasn't exactly heavy I just knew I would have to use it and that's what was creating the real weight in my hand. We didn't have a plan and I didn't have a signal to give him, so I decided the best plan of attack was to just attack.

I lunged at the first guy in front of me, slicing the knife through the air and since they were not trained killers, they weren't dodging as well as they should have been. Granted I wasn't a trained killer either, but I'd used a knife before. I could feel Cyrus fighting someone from behind me and I only hoped he had some sort of weapon. Granted, he could just give into his animalistic instincts and use his teeth.

The guy I started out fighting, had me by the arm and was going for my throat trying to knock me out. Bringing my elbow back hard, I got him square in the nose. It gushed out like a broken pipe, spraying blood all over my shoulder. His hands dropped from around me to tend to his nose and I went for the next guy.

I swung my head over to where I heard a loud and vibrating scream or growl, I wasn't quite sure what it was, but I knew it came from Cyrus. Finding where he was, I turned in time to see him yanking his fangs out of the throat of some guy he was fighting.

Seeing that he was taking care of himself, I focused on what I was supposed to do, whipping my head back around I came in contact with a fist. Feeling and hearing his knuckles making contact with my face and more importantly, my nose, I stepped back, stunned. Blinking my eyes and gingerly touching my nose, I found that it was bleeding profusely, and it probably wouldn't stop for a while.

My head was spinning some and when I finally got my footing back and wiped my eyes from the water and some blood, only to see Gregory standing in front of me. "Looks like someone grew a new pair and is ready to fight again. Well bring it on, let's get this over with." I was getting tired and dizzy from the headache forming from being punched in the face.

If you had told me a few months ago that I would be fighting Gregory Rice in the field next to an abandoned castle with a person that was older than some of the dirt around here, I would have laughed and called you crazier than crazy bread, but here I was, fists held high with grass stains on my butt and a bloody nose. "You should have just stayed out of this, Henny. You would have been safe." I glared at him, no one called me that. "Drop dead, Gregg." I practically spat at him.

I rushed him, catching him off guard and laid a right-handed punch to his jaw. He stumbled back a bit but composed himself quickly. He came for me and while I ducked out of the way of his left hand coming for my left side-distracted, I missed the swift punch to my gut from his right hand. He knocked the wind out of me and I stumbled back, but I wasn't done with him.

I got back to a stable position and grabbed for his shirt collar. I pulled him to me and with everything I had, I slammed my head into his head sufficiently knocking him out cold. I turned to Cyrus and saw that he had had his way with the rest of the guys. Blood flowed from his mouth and when he went to wipe it off more replaced it.

I walked over to him, spitting blood out of my mouth as I did. The blood from my nose was filling my mouth and making me choke a bit. I coughed up the rest of the blood that had flowed into my mouth and wiped some of the blood off my nose. "Are they dead?" I asked him through a mouth full of blood. I thought there were a few teeth that were bleeding as well. "No, I do not kill people anymore. But with all their blood in my system, I am getting a bit disoriented. Let us get back to the castle." I nodded my head in agreement and walked towards him.

I leaned on his shoulder and arm hoping my legs wouldn't give out on me. The dizziness in my head was getting worse and I needed to lay down. I started slumping over and wasn't really on his shoulder any more but before I knew it, Cyrus had swept me up into his arms and started walking towards the doors of the castle. "You fought well, perhaps I could show you a few things with a sword. I think you would do well."

He looked down at me and I nodded my head yes at him. I was going to agree to anything he said in this state anyways. At least that took care of that for a little while.

Swordsman in Training

Cyrus

Waking up to a blood curdling scream was as surprising as waking up in a soft bed again. I sprang into action, I more or less jumped out of the bed and ran to the source of the screaming. Since Henrietta was the only other living thing in the castle I assumed she was the one screaming, I just needed to get to her.

I knew she compared me to a fictional creature called a vampire, but I knew them from stories when I was little, and they had super speed. I did not. It would really come in handy right now though.

I ran down each hall, not really remembering what hallway she was in. Getting to the one closest to the front set of stairs, I turned the corner too sharp and nearly landed myself against the wall. Another scream belted out from a room down the hall I was in. Spotting the door to the room she stayed in, I bolted towards it.

I got to the door's threshold to see Henrietta still screaming and creating a restless mess in the bed she was sleeping in, or rather thrashing in.

Besides the screaming, she seemed to have her eyes closed and she was still in bed. The thought dawned on me and I realized she was having a nightmare. I used to get them when I was younger, after my mother passed, and now I get them constantly like a movie playing in my head.

Henrietta told me about movies and I was curious to actually see one, but we could always do that later. Right now, I needed to wake her up. I walked towards the bed and studied her movements as I did. It was like she was trying to fight someone off. I wondered if it had anything to do with the fight a couple of nights ago.

I knew her nose had healed, and nothing was broken, even the tooth she thought came out was fine, maybe this was about something else. I sat on the edge of the bed and attempted to gently wake her up. It was no easy task.

Her arm swung up and nearly got me in the face, the other one was about to do the same until I stopped it. I gently held both her arms down and watched her body try to move while being restrained. Her torso moved up and down trying to get herself free, all while she was still asleep. "Henrietta, wake up. You need to wake up…" I took her by the shoulders and shook her a little bit. Her head rolled from one side to another before her eyes began to flutter open.

Her eyes looked around the room and then landed on me. She gave off a confused look like she was not sure if she was still dreaming or not. "Cyrus… wh–what are you doing in here, holding my shoulders, sitting on the bed while I'm sleeping…" She looked around the room and at me and then the room again. "You were screaming in your sleep. I came in to see if you were okay." I knew it would be bad to get attached to someone like her. Someone young and with a full life ahead of them. I had lived too long and if I got my curse broken then that should be it, I should die a free man. Regardless I should die in the end, completely, I did not know what I would do if I could not achieve that. "Oh, well… thanks but it was just a dream." She shrugged her shoulders and avoided eye contact with me. Something else was going on and she needed her mind off of it. "I have an idea, when I have dreams such as yours, I used to fence with my instructor to get out my aggression or anything else going on. Want to give it a try, I bet you will be a natural at it." I stared at her almost not giving her an out to say no or walk away from the offer. "Yeah alright, let me get a pair of pants on and I'll meet you out there in the foyer or whatever." I took that as excitement and left the room at her request. I quickly walked to where I knew my old fencing equipment was to see if there was anything left of it.

I walked the halls up and down trying to remember where that old closet was. It had been so long since I explored this place, but I also knew that they did not take everything out of here when it closed down. Finding nearly a tenth hallway or at least what I thought was a tenth one, I quickly ran down it and stopped when I found something particularly interesting.

It was not my fencing gear, but it would work none the less. I grabbed the gear and took it to the foyer where I hoped she was already waiting. I got to the stairs and looked over the railing to see her with her arms crossed waiting for me. I decided to start her off with a bit of an adrenaline rush. "Wake Up!" I shouted to her and threw down one of the pieces to our training. She whipped around and caught the flying piece of metal in her hand before I knew it. She was better than I could have imagined but let us see how good she really is.

I walked down the steps in a light trot and when I made it to the bottom, I was met with a confused face. "I thought you said fencing, this is a bit heavier than a fencing foil you know because it's a real fucking sword, Cyrus." I was not sure if she was doing the sarcastic thing she tried to tell me about, or if she was mad. "This is supposed to take your mind off whatever was making you scream in your sleep. Plus, seeing your moves the other night made me think you had a knack for this." I drew her to the middle of the foyer with the other sword in my hand. "I used these swords to spar with my tutors and with people I thought needed to be fought. You know how I was... before, I was crazy and thought everyone needed to be fought with swords." I shrugged my shoulders and began to circle her with my sword.

Not really looking at her while I did so, instead I got the feel of the room and the sword in my hand. The weight in my hand felt familiar like I had used it yesterday. The sheen of the sword was dull and so was the blade. They had not been taken care of.

I looked up to see her in a stance that looked like she had spared before. "Before you ask, yes I have done something similar to this before. The UK is a lot different from schools in America, even if I only went to one for like a minute. But... when I came here, they offered fencing in school and took it and did rather well. So, you may have a real fight on your hands. Or at least a couple of years of experience against you." She smiled at me with her crooked grin and I took my stance in front of her. "Then let us begin." Slipping my left arm behind my back as she did with hers, I lunged at her. She stepped back, quickly dodging my blade. I knew I would not do much damage since the blade was dull, it would bruise more than cut at this point.

I watched her wrist as she swung the blade in her hand letting the blade swing through the air next to her. She was about to make a move.

I stepped forward again and this time instead of taking a step back, she lunged at me as I did to her. Our swords clashed, and the sound of metal resonated through the room. She flipped around allowing her sword to swing around her body where it came in contact with mine. I took a step back as she faced forward again. She pointed her sword towards me and gave me a look.

I was not sure what the look meant, but I knew she had something planned. I took my chance and skipped my footing towards her in a lung, only this time I swung my sword from the tip of my foot up to her face only she was there in time to block it from taking its mark.

The clash of the swords gave me a small flash back to when I sparred with my tutors.

Our swords continued to clash as our feet danced with each other. I missed this, the dance of swords, metal on metal fighting. I missed being able to go up against someone that was worthy of my skills and time.

I only hoped for more of this.

Family Ties

Henrietta

My arm was completely sore from sparring with Cyrus yesterday, but I was happy that I won. Well… we tied but I'm counting it as a win.

I untangled myself from the blankets and scooting myself up to the headboard of the bed, trying to wake up more. I rubbed my shoulder while I rotated it a bit so that it stretched out some without hurting myself. Stretching out the rest of my upper body, I looked around the room for the hundredth time, only this time something was off.

I swung my legs off the bed and touched them to the cold stone floor beneath me. I only wished that they had redone the floors like they had a few other things like the bathtubs and stuff. I should have brought socks with me.

That was something I wanted to ask him about, not socks, but visiting my house down the hill. I missed my sister a lot and I needed to tell her that everything was okay. I hated being away from her but it wasn't like I missed her company even though I did, it was that I left her with a barely treated wound on her neck and a note saying I would return when everything was over.

I walked around the room and noticed that my bag had seemed to explode everywhere. Usually, I kept a tidy room, except for clothes on the ground, but this was like a disaster zone. I didn't even think I had brought this much stuff, but I guess when I grabbed my go bag that I always had stored in the hall closet at my house, just in case I needed to get somewhere fast, I didn't remember that there was this much stuff.

I gently moved a few things around with my toe and when I did, I saw that something was broken underneath some of my things.

I bent down and moved some more things around to find where the broken glass was from. I dug around and found nothing that was made of glass or would have had glass on it. I tossed a piece into the trash bin near the door and when I looked up Cyrus was in the door way. Again. "You know every time I seem to wake up in the afternoon, because we can't do anything during the day, you are either on the bed waking me up or standing in the doorway." I eyed him from the floor and watched as he continued to lean against the door frame. "I seem to be on the same sleep schedule as you are. It was bound to happen seeing as you have been staying here for nearly two months." He spoke down to me.

I stood up and faced him, trying not to step on the glass around my feet. "I had a few questions for you and I don't know if you will like them or not. But be aware that you liking them is not contingent on them happening or not." I stood my ground and I knew that he knew I always meant what I said. "Go on then." He spoke to me as he stood up straight from the doorway. "I would like to go see my sister. I mean you've kept me here from school and my only family member. I need to tell her I'm okay, I can't just sit here and act like she thinks I'm fine. I need to know. I haven't seen her face in over a month. I know you have mixed feelings about family and all that, but she is the only piece I have left. Please allow this." I was acting like he was my warden in a prison cell when we both knew that he only wanted me here to cure him and then he would leave me alone.

But asking him seemed easier than just running away and explaining later after he'd tracked me down thinking I left for good. "Can I have a say on it?" He walked into the room and over the mess to the bed. He took a seat on the bed and I waited for him to make his call on the situation. "I would like to come with you. I need to apologize to a lot of people and your sister is one of them. Please allow me to go with you." That surprised me and, in all honesty, I didn't think he would be like this.

He wasn't the same person that attacked my sister just to get me back to the castle, there was still a bit of that in there, but he's grown a lot too. "That works for me, by the way do you know what broke in here that was glass?" Maybe he knew why there was random shards of glass on the ground. "Oh, I um, took something from your house the first time and it broke the other day. Here!" He handed me a folded piece of paper and I took it.

Unfolding the thick paper, I saw that it was a picture of my sister and me. It was the day she won a chairman's award for her robotics with her team. This was one of the best days, we got to go into the country next to us and she got to show off her skills. She really is an amazing robotics engineer. "You stole a picture? I'm assuming the frame broke and that's what's on my floor." I looked up at him from the photo and saw that his face was down in what I can only assume was sadness. "I took it when I first entered the house. When your sister called out for you, I knew that what I was going to do would be wrong, but I did it anyways. So I took the photo to remind myself to stop and to make myself feel bad later about it. I am sorry the frame broke." He sounded like a sad three-year-old.

I wanted to be mad at him and I *was* mad at him, but at the same time, I could see him fighting with himself to do better and to fix what he'd done in the past. "Alright! You can come with me."

We were half way to my house when he started to have a sneezing fit. It was multiple sneezes in a row and it was contagious because I started sneezing as well. Usually, I didn't have allergies but with the wind blowing around us, I must have picked something up.

We had to stop at the end of my street so that we could compose ourselves before our next sneezing fit. I wiped my eyes from the tears that the oncoming allergies gave me, and tried to stand up straight, but laughing at Cyrus wasn't helping. "Have you never had allergies before? Because your sneeze face is hilarious." I stopped laughing long enough to help him to a more upright position. He wiped his eyes down as well and composed himself. "I have never sneezed so much in my whole life, I think there is something that we are both allergic to." He made a good point. "The only thing I'm allergic to are poppies. I break out if I touch them and if I'm around them, then I sneeze just like this." I looked around us but couldn't find much in the dark. "I am allergic to poppy flowers too. What are the odds?" He smiled at me and started for the house again. I followed behind him, wondering about the odds as well.

We walked a few more blocks down and finally got to my house. It looked the same and even if it had only been a couple of months I thought it would look different. I shrugged my shoulders and dug around in my pocket for the key.

Finding it quickly I stuck it in the keyhole and turned it for good measure. Hearing the click that told me it was unlocked. I turned the doorknob and took in a big breath at the same time. Opening the door, I took in the living room with the lights on and the TV turned to the cooking channel; she was home.

I walked into the room and felt Cyrus right behind me. I knew she would be in the kitchen or maybe her room but when I heard the squeaking from the staircase, I turned my head to see my sister standing at the top. Her eyes went wide, and she ran to me nearly tripping on the stair in the process. "Oh my, Henri, I thought you would never come back." She clung onto me and gave me the biggest hug I had ever received. "I told you I wouldn't be gone forever, but I do have someone here that wants to tell you something." I pulled away from her and moved over a bit so that Cyrus could come into the light. "Oh my god! What is he doing here?" She sounded frightened like there was something other than the fact he nearly killed her going on. She had always been skittish around people that hurt her, or that she got a bad 'vibe' from. My parents ruined more than her mind when we were growing up. "He's here to apologize, for hurting you and for being the reason that I left in the first place." I went ahead and told her quickly why we were there. "He can't be here." Her eyes were locked on Cyrus and I wasn't sure why she was so wigged out. Usually, she was wary about people like Cyrus, or really anyone new in our lives but she didn't act like this, she tried to hide what she felt for the most part and then she freaked out later. "What's going on, Olivia?" I asked her while she began backing up the staircase. "She's here, she's in the house and she wants him dead. She's using me Henri, using me to get to you. You shouldn't have come here." Her eyes switched from me to the top of the staircase, but what grabbed my attention first was the other person coming down the stairs behind her. "She's right, you know. You shouldn't have come home, Henri." Margaret stood behind my sister and before I could move a muscle, she put a gun to her head.

Fool Me Once

I watched the gun up against my sister's temple and internally I was screaming, how could she have fooled me again? This time it was much worse, she had my sister in a dangerous situation and I swore, even if she was older than me, I would never let her get into a situation like this again. I protected her after we left my parents because she couldn't be strong anymore. She broke down a few months after moving here when she saw something familiar in our house or on the TV, every time she was triggered, I was there to help her, to protect her; now I had failed.

Anger flowed through my veins as my eyes turned to Margaret who was holding the gun. My sister was keeping her cool and not shaking like she should be. But that was us, keeping our cool under high amounts of stress and danger and then breaking down later when no one could see. I guess that could be our superpower or something. "Margaret, when are you going to learn you can't scare me. We all know you aren't going to kill her, you've probably never shot a gun before. Let's call this a night and talk it over some more tomorrow. Because Margaret, you do not want to piss me off." I was done with her, her and Gregory but he was a different story. "You think you could even lay a finger on me. I'm over three centuries old, you can't touch me!" She was yelling at an abnormally loud level for indoors and it really pushed my buttons. I didn't want to make a move with the gun still at her temple and because they were on a staircase, so many things could go wrong like one false move and they fall down the stairs, gun and all. "Margaret, it is me you want, it was I that killed your brother and ruined your life. Let her sister go and you can point the gun at me. Killing her will only make Henrietta angrier and then that will make me furious. Let Her. Go." Cyrus was spewing threats behind me while I couldn't take my eyes off her and the gun.

I watched my sister's eyes this time, waiting for her to tell me something. Not with her words of course but growing up with my particular parents we learned to speak in other ways than with our mouths. I watched her eyes waiting for them to speak to me. And with a glare she told me to get the hell out of there, but I wasn't going to start listening to her now. I'd seen someone disarm another person before, I watched a lot of TV, but could I do it in real life? I guess we were going to find out.

Just like when I was sparring with Cyrus, I absentmindedly slipped my left arm behind my back and quickly lunged at her and the gun and in one quick, nearly unseen move, I smacked the gun holding hand from below sufficiently getting her to loosen her grip enough for the gun to fly into the wall behind it.

The stunned look on Margaret, Olivia and Cyrus' faces made me smile. I knew they weren't expecting that. "Like I said Margaret, you are bad with guns. Now back away from my sister before the next hit is to your head." I gave her a smug look and before I knew it, she was shouting at me, words that I was unfamiliar with. "Projiciet!" She shouted at me and as soon as the word was spoken, it was like I had been punched in the gut hard enough to fling me across the room and into the wall above the fireplace. I fell to the ground and when I finally got air back into my lungs, I started to get up off the ground.

Well, if she had that up her sleeve why did she use the gun? "Is that the best you got, little witch." I knew taunting someone that could use magic against me was a bad idea, but really it was all I had at the moment. "You are a fool Henrietta, and you will die knowing that." She began towards me and away from my sister, I gave a quick look to Cyrus and luckily, he knew what it meant. He quickly got to my sister and took her upstairs and away from the mess that was about to happen. "Fool me once shame on you, try to fool me twice and I'll have you in a grave before you can mutter a single word." I gave her the 'come and get it' hand gesture, I was ready to get this over with.

My head was still ringing from the throw she gave me, but I was still standing on two feet. I could do this. I looked her right in the eyes and suddenly felt the room grow a bit colder and I knew she had something to do with it. "Changing the AC temp, really? Wow! I thought you were supposed to be some big powerful witch, but I guess you're a bit rusty." There I go with the taunting again.

I glanced up to see Cyrus at the top of the stairs again, he bent down for a second and then came back into view, and I knew we had her. I just needed to keep distracting her. I also knew that Cyrus wouldn't know how to shoot a gun, and even if it was a bit obvious, he would still need help, I on the other hand have shot plenty of guns. "You think you're all big and bad because of the way you were raised and the parents you had. Well boohoo your history was tragic. Try growing up in the 1600s and living through four hundred more years. Try living with a mother that ignored you and did everything to get more power. It was a nightmare." She was going off on a tangent, just like the bad guys in movies when they start their monologue. "Look, I'm not trying to sell my back story here, I'm just trying to get you out of the picture and break whatever your dumb ass mother did to him. He made mistakes and we all know that. Hell! He knows that. But she should not have tortured him with the memories of his dead mother. She should not have drove him to madness over the death of her son. She should have mourned the loss, told the proper authorities, and had him tried at the time, whether he was the prince or not. I read the books and I know his father would have punished him."

I was matched in a staring contest and I wasn't sure if I was winning. "This isn't about my dead brother any more, it was barely about him then. This is about getting what he truly deserves and that is to see all of his loved ones die. Just like I had to do." She looked me dead in the eye when she said that, and I wasn't completely sure about what she meant. "He has watched all of his loved ones die, his mother, newborn sister, he was even around when his father died. Your mother took all that away from him and yet you think he deserves more for what he did while under your mother's influence." I shook my head partly in rage, partly in annoyance. "Attrahunt." The word left her mouth before either of us could tell what she was doing. In a second, the gun that was in Cyrus' hand zoomed out of it and into her grasp instead. It was like a magnet. "He has not watched all the people he loves die yet." She held the gun in front of me and before I was able to rush towards her to stop what she was about to do and even before Cyrus could get to her from the bottom of the stairs, she pulled the trigger and emptied a round into my chest.

Shot Through the Heart

Cyrus

The blast that sent Henrietta into the wall behind her made me jump. I had never heard something like that, it was so close to a canon but so much smaller. I took no time in grabbing the witch by the head. One hand on the back of her head and the other on her chin and in one swift jerk, I snapped her neck.

The witch fell to the floor, but I was unsure if she was really dead or not, I did not know how to really kill a witch.

I heard something from upstairs and I knew it was her sister probably screaming for someone to tell her what happened, but I did not have time for that. It was luck that I knew how to lock the door so that she did not just come out of the room while her sister battled the witch.

Hearing the gasps for air from my left, I broke out of the stare I had going on with the out of sort witch on the ground. I turned to my left and quickly led myself down to my knees. Henrietta was shaking against the wall with her hand covering her chest. Dark red blood seeped from her in between her fingers.

I carefully grabbed her shoulders and tried to take the weight of her and allowed her to lean against me as I sat more on the ground instead of my knees. I was unfamiliar with a wound like this, so I did the only thing I thought to do but I was interrupted before I could. "Henny! Is she okay? Did that bitch shoot her?" Olivia practically screamed from the stairs, but I did not see her rush over to us. She stayed on the stairs and I could see her shaking from where I was, I only assumed she broke the lock to the door, so she could get out. "We need to get her to a hospital, now! This gunshot looks like it is incredibly close to her heart. Can you pick her up without moving her too much?" I was not listening to her, not on purpose I was just

161

distracted. Her sister must have come to her senses enough to tell me what to do.

I watched the now much paler than usual Henrietta with the light that had nearly gone from her eyes. I held her chin up with my index finger and made her face look to me. Her eyes opened and closed slowly and her hand that was covering the wound on her chest began to become weak and slip from its place.

My hearing was going in and out, and it finally picked up on what Olivia was trying to tell me. "Bring her to the car and hurry." I looked up in time to see her sister bolt out the door and to her car. I snapped out of my worry and laced my arm under her folded legs and then put the other behind her back.

I lifted her up as carefully as possible and when I got her to my chest, she let out a small grunt of pain. I stopped as soon as she made a noise, I did not want to hurt her more. I leaned my mouth down to her ear and whispered soft things to her. Hoping it would calm her down some. "You will be alright, I will make sure of it." I laid a kiss to her now cold forehead and headed to the car.

I had never been in a car before and I did not like it. Surrounded by metal that was currently flying down the road and through the town. I held onto Henrietta more and more for my own needs as the car went faster and faster. This was a death trap and I did not see why people liked using them. Give me a horse any day.

I watched the blood that was still coming from her chest fall on the car's seat and realizing that her hand was not there anymore I replaced it with mine so that maybe some of the blood would stop coming out.

I only hoped the healers of this day were better than the ones of mine.

When the death trap car came to an abrupt stop and I nearly went into the front seat by sheer force. "Okay, we're here, let's get her inside. Quickly." She spoke to me from the front seat as she got out of the car and helped me with my door.

I carried Henrietta as I had before and found that she was growing more and more limp. Her sister burst through the doors of a bright and shiny building. I guess healers were much better now than they had been.

I took a quick look around and tried to ignore the stares coming from the people that were here before us and instead followed her sister as she tried to get the attention of a healer. "Please help my sister, she's been shot!" She screamed for someone to help us and every time someone came to help they took a look at me and they ran in the opposite direction. I hated that the way I looked was getting in the middle of her getting help.

I stole one of the beds in the hall and placed her on it quickly and then I let her sister take over from there. I decided that it would be best if I stood in the shadows of the whole process. I watched as the people wearing white jackets take her away on the bed I had laid her on.

Her sister looked back at me for a second and then ran after where they were taking her sister. I thought for a moment that maybe she wanted me to go with her but of course, that would be absurd. I would be better off at the castle like I always have been.

Henrietta

Foggy, everything was foggy. My mind, my eyes, even my inner monologue. Foggy. My eyes began to peel open as a very bright light tried to push its way in further. A faint beep started out in my ear and it kept its rhythm. Beep. Beep. Beep. It was annoying.

I finally got my eyes all the way open and when I did, I saw that the room I was in smelled and looked very clean. Must be a hospital. Okay try and remember the last thing that happened before you were put into the uncomfortable hospital gown and hooked up to annoying monitors.

Then it hit me, Margaret shot me. That witch shot me! The beeping increased as my anger did and in a second I felt a hand on my cold arm. Come to think of it, my whole body was cold. "Calm down Henri, you're safe now. Stop making things beep." It was my sister. She was here with me. But what about... "Cy. Cyrus, where is he?" I asked her as I gently sat up and looked around the room. I didn't see him anywhere and I hoped he was okay. It was dark when we had gotten to the house, but I also didn't know how long I had been out for. There was a tightness in my chest when I moved, forcing me to stay down instead.

"He just left, I think it was because people kept looking at him. How are you feeling?"

How was I feeling? I felt like killing that witch and finding out if Cyrus was okay. But now that I started moving around a bit more, I was feeling a bit of pain.

I looked down at the bandage on my chest that was underneath the gown and saw that it was larger than expected. "The bullet missed your heart but there was some damage to the vessels and stuff like that, but they assured me that they fixed it all. Only took like five hours but they fixed you up." She had tears in her eyes and I couldn't blame her. If she had been the one that was shot, I would be a mess right now.

There had been only one other time that one of us had been this bad and it required surgery and it was Olivia that was hurt. I had been eleven at the time and I didn't keep it together at all.

I needed to make sure he was okay, but I knew she wasn't going to let me out of her site after this. "Can you get me some water? Please?" I asked as sweetly as possible and waited for her to leave the room.

Throwing the covers off my body and swinging my legs to the edge of the bed, I got stopped. Looking at my hand I saw that I was hooked up to an IV. Great, this wasn't going to feel very good. I grasped the plastic piece on the top of my hand and then held my breath for good measure, then I gave it a quick yank and a shock of pain went through me.

I covered the tiny hole it left behind and then stepped onto the floor. I didn't have time to get dressed so I grabbed some slippers and the robe on the edge of my bed and tried the window in the room. Finding the lock, I clicked it open and propped the window open just enough for me to squeeze myself through the opening. Every move I made felt like I was being stabbed in my heart.

I harshly fell into the bush that was under my window and when I got my footing back, I had to hold the spot over my chest wound. This wasn't a good idea after all. A lot of pain hit me all at once and I started to get sick, holding back the urge to barf, I made my way out of the bush.

I wish I had my scooter right now and I had been wishing that the entire walk to the castle. It was much longer when you were on the other side of the town, barefoot, and had just come out of surgery and had a large stitched up wound on my chest.

But the more I walked even with the pain and nausea, I still came to see the castle in the distance. It was just a little bit further. I took a look back in the direction of the castle and hoped that Olivia would understand I needed to be with him. The great big door was a welcome this time and instead of opening it properly like with my hand or something, I just sort of leaned on it and hoped it would open for me anyways. I really needed to lay down. My head was becoming foggy again and the pain hadn't let up for a single second.

The creak of the door led me to the front foyer and when I leaned my back against the back of the door to close it, I slid down it until my butt hit the floor. The feel of even and solid ground underneath me felt nice. Now, I needed to know if my walk here was worth the pain. "Cyrus!" I yelled his name and waited for him to show his face. I heard the rough almost gravel sound of my voice bouncing off the walls as I waited for him to come to my aid.

I was tired though, even if I had disconnected the drug solution I was still feeling the effects. I saw the shadow of a figure come towards me as my eyes began to shut in defeat of the lack of drugs flowing through my system. At least, the pain was starting to die down since everything was going numb from it.

Decebal Arrives

Waking up to a big soft bed was the least of my worries at the moment, at the moment there was blood leaking from my bandage on my chest and an incredible pain coming from the same spot. I couldn't get off the bed very well and I didn't know if screaming in the early evening was appropriate at the moment.

But what the hell. "CYRUS!" I screamed his name hoping he was actually in the building because all I remembered was getting into the castle and passing out from the pain in my chest, I barely remembered if he came to my aid or not. I assumed he did since I was in the bed I'd been using. "You are awake, that is good to see." He rubbed his eyes like I had woken him from a deep slumber. But I needed help. "Um, I'm having a bit of trouble here, it seems my stitches have popped and I'm bleeding again." I pointed to my chest and I saw his eyes go down to my chest to see the blood for himself and if he could blush then he would be right now. I knew I was. "Right, let us get you to the bathroom then." He walked quickly to the bed and helped me to my feet. Things had been feeling different since the whole Margaret attack, but I'll let it just roll off my shoulder for right now. I'll try and be ignorant for the moment because what I felt when he carried me into the hospital last night for the small amount I kept waking up and passing back out, and when he helped me out of bed just now. Better off ignoring until it comes up again, that's my motto.

Cyrus helped me to the bathroom closest to the room I was in. When we entered the bathroom, I waddled over to the counter being careful not to jostle myself around too much.

I sat on the counter and used the last of my medic supplies from my go bag. I peeled the soiled bandage off my chest and cleaned the area. The water stung a bit and I thought it was just because the nerve underneath the skin that was cut up from the surgery were messed up. The numbness from the medicine they had given me had worn off and it wasn't just pressure pain I was feeling anymore, it was pure nerve pain now and it hurt so badly.

I flinched as my finger came into more contact with my skin and as I went to reach for a new piece of gauze, I saw it held in front of my face before I could. "Thanks, and also thank you for taking me from the foyer last night when I stupidly ran from the hospital, the place with the pain killers and everything." I looked down at the gauze and place it on where the stitches were just sort of hanging on. I took the medical tape and kept the gauze in place while I taped around the border of the incision. I had to make sure that my shirt didn't slip down too far because I wasn't wearing a bra. "What do you mean? I did not take you to that room. Margaret did." I nearly choked on my own spit. "WHAT DO YOU MEAN MARGARET DID?" I was so furious that I nearly let my entire shirt fall the rest of the way down, he allowed her back into our lives after she SHOT me? "Please listen to me, Henrietta." I wasn't having any of this. I jumped down from the counter and put my shirt back into place. I stormed out of the bathroom as much as I could while still being hurt. It probably looked hilarious. "You need to listen to what I have to say." I could hear him yelling after me but I didn't want to hear it.

I got back to the room and started packing my bags, all the junk on the floor and everything. I wanted out of here, I didn't want to see his face again. How could he have allowed her to be around him or me after everything she did? "If you will not talk back to me, then just listen. I went back to your house to see if I had killed her or not and she was there just waiting for me. It was her mother the whole time and by that, I mean, her mother has been watching her and if she had not gotten mad at me for the death of her brother and then mad at you for getting in the way she would have come here sooner than planned." I stopped cleaning my junk up and listened to what he was saying. "How do I know it's all true? And what do you mean by sooner than planned and how did she listen to her?" I had so many questions and the pain in my chest was getting worse, I felt like I was having a heart attack. "It was a spell, just come

167

with me to the back room and she can show you. We do not have much time, Decebal is coming." He held a hand out for me and I figured that if Margaret tried anything that I could just stab her with the knife I had slipped into my pocket earlier.

I only took his hand because I was having trouble standing up as it was. Before he walked with me, I picked up a shirt and a pair of sweatpants and quickly put them on, nearly falling after not getting my pants on right the first time. The shirt was harder to get on over the hospital gown and then I had to pull the gown out though the sleeve of my night shirt. He guided me from the bedroom to the back room which I had not had the pleasure of seeing yet, which also meant it was not cleaned. Most of the castle still wasn't, I mean I knew it was mine and all but I really didn't care right now if it was clean or not.

When we entered the room, I saw Margaret standing in the middle of a ring of candles with a guilt-stricken face. We'll just see how guilty she really is. I let his hand go and stood in the archway of the room, I wasn't getting any closer to her. "Before you jump on the kill Margaret bandwagon let me tell you that I'm sorry for everything. That person you met when you first moved here is the real me, the one that's been making an appearance the last month or so is the one that's controlled by my mother. She put a spell on me when she left the country after she cursed him. If I was ever in contact with the prince then she would know that it was time to come here, she would know that he had been released and since the room was lined with iron she wasn't able to keep tabs on him in there just when he was released, through me. And when she knows that he's out, she will break the part of the curse that keeps him bound to the castle." I looked at her and didn't accept her apology, I wasn't buying into anything yet. Mainly because we sort of found a way around the whole leaving the castle thing. "And the day you told me about my brother, which I already knew about by the way, I told myself that I needed to push you and him away from me so that my mother doesn't intervene, that she saw I was just as mad at you as she was. But it's too late, she's coming and she's going to unleash the prince on the town and then the rest of the world. She can control him." Those last words got my attention, I wasn't going to let anything happen to him when I'd promised him I would help find his cure. And

168

probably for another reason that I was ignoring right now. "Say I believe you, how much time do we have to break the curse and get him away from your mother?" She looked relieved that I was talking to her, but I wasn't buying into anything yet. "The curse is complicated and I'm not sure if I really know how to do it and as for time –" "You are out of it. Time, that is." a booming voice came from above us and all around the room at the same time, cutting Margaret off mid-sentence and when I looked at her I saw her physically shaking with fear, I knew what it meant to fear a parent. "She's here, Decebal is here." I quickly walked over to where Cyrus was standing and stood in front of him. I may have a sown-up hole above my heart but that wasn't going to stop me from protecting what I cared about.

Stopping mid-thought, I looked behind me at Cyrus, who was looking around the room waiting for the witch to make her appearance. Did I care about Cyrus that much? The thought about it was making my head spin a bit or that was the small amount of blood I lost this morning.

Before I could think about anything else, the room began to shake and move and before my eyes, a bright light blasted through the room and when Cyrus' arms wrapped around my head shielding my eyes. When the light died down, I looked at the figure in the middle of the room and before my eyes stood the witch that started this all. "Decebal." My voice rang through the room like it was empty and bouncing off the walls. The witch turned to me and as her deep green eyes stared into mine, I felt the sting of the bullet wound fresh under my skin once again.

You're to Blame

The air in the room went cold after the energy around the witch settled. It was like a dead body entering a room. If a dead body could walk obviously, and I don't mean a zombie because I was pretty sure zombie would be unnaturally warm. But let's got back to what was happening in front of me.

I could feel Cyrus on edge behind me and I couldn't do much about it. I was trapped by the witch's stare, her deep green eyes looked into my soul. When I was finally able to break contact with her and look around the room, I saw all the dust fly around; fairy dust was everywhere.

I thought back to the summoning book we stole from Margaret. Looks like that ended up being a waste of time and an unnecessary bloody nose. Although, I did get to pound on Gregory, so that was the plus side.

I looked over at Decebal who was capturing the room with her presence. Her dark red hair blew over her shoulder from a breeze that came from nowhere. I could feel the power coming from her, but I wasn't going to let that scare me. I had a bullet wound in my chest and I left my sister at the hospital, I wasn't here to just stare at someone, I was here to kick ass.

I looked over at Margaret to see a face filled with utter fear. She was dead scared of her mother. She was four hundred and something years old! She shouldn't be scared of her mother. But feeling the vibe that was coming off of her I could understand a little bit.

She watched the room and when her eyes went back to Cyrus behind me, I scooted back to him a bit, trying to tell her to stay away from him. "Well what do we have here? Someone is out of their cage, and just in time too. And on the other side of the room we have a traitor in our midst. Did you really think I would buy that whole 'turning against them' idea you had? I was not born yesterday, Margaret." Decebal spoke coldly to her daughter on the other side of the room.

Her eyes kept going around the room looking at the various pieces of old art and the dust collection. I noticed that she didn't even think to look at me after she got here. She was ignoring me for a reason. I wasn't going to have any of that, screw her and her magic. "Hey, old lady! You think you can just show up here and start handing out guilt cards? Look around, no one is scared of you. Not even Margaret. Right?" I looked towards Margaret and tried to give her a bit of confidence.

She looked back at me and I saw her mood shift a bit. She had been held down by her mother for four hundred years and I was feeling guilty for not seeing it sooner. I had been oppressed and taken down by my mother for too many years. I knew she shot me but she was trying to protect us as well and I thought that might just win me over in the end. I mean if I could forgive Cyrus for what he had done to my sister and me, then I thought I'd eventually forgive her. Just give me time.

Decebal looked at me finally and I nearly ate my words. She was pure evil, and I seriously didn't know how Margaret had dealt with her when she was young and still living with her mother. I mean my mother was evil, and so was my father, there is no way around that. But they didn't have access to magic and they still made a huge impact on my life and others around us. I was in between the idea of who of the three of them were the evillest. "She's right, mother, you are nothing but a bully, a badly dressed one at that. You haven't changed your style of clothes since the 1800s. But that's not important. You're going to take the curse off of him because we both know what really happened that day." I looked at her with a confused look. "What really happened? What do you mean, Margaret?" Cyrus spoke up from behind me and without realizing that he had his hands on my shoulders for a while now. He sounded confused but at the same time he didn't seemed scared of her at all. "If you aren't going to tell them then I shall." Margaret spoke back to her mother and when she did, Decebal crossed her arms and gave her a 'I dare you to' look. "It was her from the beginning like I had told you before. But what I didn't say was that even my brother being killed was her idea. She sent him down there to try and rile the prince up. She of course didn't know that you would kill him but in the end, she didn't care. She just wanted your mind in a dark place. The spell to make you crazy would be a lot easier to perform if you were." Cyrus' grip on my shoulders became tighter, he was upset obviously. "Don't say another word Margaret. Or else." Decebal threatened Margaret in front of us both. "Or else what mother? You'll set me up to die like you did with Aaron that day? Or curse me to do your bidding in the end like you're doing with Cyrus? He had his life before him and you ruined it. He could have grieved and then moved on like he was supposed to, but you had to be there to make him go insane. He would have been a great king!" Her shouts were probably heard from the bottom of the hill.

I looked up at Cyrus and saw that he was staring dead on at the witch. If I didn't watch him, he was going to start something too soon and got hurt. "Let's just see about that. CYRUS!" She shouted and before I could think of turning to stop him from doing anything, I felt the grip of Cyrus fall off my shoulders. I turned around to see what he was doing, and my voice caught in my throat.

His face was straight forward like he wasn't looking at anything at all, his eyes were fixed on something and when I followed them I saw that they were locked on Decebal in the middle of the room. As I watched his eyes, I saw the veins darken under his skin and pull into his eyes. I wasn't scared because I'd seen it before, but I was worried, he seemed trapped under Decebal's control. "Now, let us see how mighty this knight of yours is; the cursed shall fight the knight to the death. And then we shall move to the rest of the town." Decebal's command hit Cyrus like a sledgehammer and I watched as he walked towards her, ignoring my tug on his arm as he did. When Margaret said he was going to be under her control, she wasn't lying. "I'm not a knight!" I shouted towards her. I was tired of being called that. If anything, I was just a lowly high school student that probably won't graduate this year.

I looked at Margaret as she did something behind her mother's back. In a moment the ring of candles lit up around her and I watched her mumble something under her breath. I ignored her for the moment and turned my attention to the other witch in the room. Cyrus was standing next to her like he was her soldier and I hated that he didn't have any control over his mind right now. Seeing him like this made me want to run her through with a sword.

When I heard the mumbling stop over by where Margaret was hosting a burning man festival, I tingling feeling went through my hand. When I looked down, there was a long and shiny metal sword appearing right before my eyes, and before I knew it the weight of a full length fighting sword was in my hand. I knew what I had to do. I was going to fight Cyrus until I found a way to kill Decebal and got him back from her. I wasn't going to let him be used by that witch; here goes everything.

The Prince's Knight

I pulled my thumb over the hilt of the shining sword in my hand, the black jewel at the tip of it by the end of my palm sparked in the candle light as I turned it slightly. I looked down the stretch of the blade and saw that it had engravings on it, but they weren't in a language I was familiar with. The blade was sharper than what I was used to, but I needed all the help when it came to fighting a Decebal controlled Cyrus.

I knew I'd sparred with him but when I say I won, I was over extending my abilities, what I meant was we tied but he was just a bit better than me, and in a life or death situation I would need every bit of extra talent I could pull out of my ass at the moment. I only hoped him being under her spell would make him a bit worse than usual. But when I saw that Decebal had done something similar for Cyrus as Margaret did for me, only his magically enhanced sword was bigger.

I took in a gulp of air and gave Margaret a glance. I saw that she had her nose in a book and I knew that she needed this distraction. Her mom finding out that she was trying to break the curse was a bad, bad idea, so fighting him may just be the distraction she needed. I only hoped she hurried.

I walked closer to Cyrus and when his black eyes descended on to mine, a shiver ran through me. Usually, the black eyes and veins didn't stir me at all, but to think that his mind was gone too was something else entirely. "Cyrus, I know you can hear me, at least I hope you can. I didn't believe that I could be anything other than the product of my parents, my sister is a genius and so were my parents, regardless of their actions. Now, I see what I was meant to do, I'm meant to protect you, you may be a lot stronger than me and older, but I'm going to fix everything. I will be your knight, and I will let no more harm come to you." Before I moved closer to him to begin my stance, I felt the familiar tingles from before go around my torso and legs. I looked down to see the same glittery sparks I saw when the sword appeared in my hand. Only this time a more form fitting spandex suit covered my body and then a light plastic material covered my torso, elbows, kneecaps, and shoulders.

I looked over at Margaret and gave her a silent thanks, here goes everything.

It was like a flashback to when we sparred in the foyer, I took the same stance, and so did he. It seemed as though even when you are under a mind-controlled spell, your muscle memories still remain. Instead of him taking the first move, I decided to be bold and lunged at him first even though I knew that it was a dumb move.

Our new swords clashed together, and literal sparks flew, I wasn't sure if that was a good thing, but I wasn't going to be bothered by it. He shoved me back with his sword and the force knocked me to the ground. I figured he was holding back the first time we fought but I wasn't aware it was this much. I quickly got up from the ground and realized he was so much stronger than me. I wasn't sure I stood a chance any more.

Swinging the sword in my hand allowing my wrist to rotate with it. My wrists always got too tight when I used a sword, or a foil which is so much lighter than this damn thing. My arm would be killing me after today, if I survived that is. His eyes never left mine and I could see my reflection in them, I looked scared.

I didn't feel scared and I hated that I looked the opposite of the way I felt. His breathing was harsh, and I could hear it from where I stood, he was trying to fight it. I swung at him again and he just barely missed my blade as it swung in front of his face. I really didn't want to hurt him but if I was going to play this off properly then I needed to make a dent in something.

His blade came towards my face and I nearly got sliced, I needed to stop thinking so much and just fight the fight in front of me. When I side stepped to the left, I missed the part where he swung his sword that way and instead of dodging it like I should have, I took the blade to the side of my stomach.

I felt the dig of the sharp edge of his sword slice over my skin. I groaned in pain and held my side. The black spandex

175

was sliced along with my skin. It wasn't deep, but it stung badly. I brought my hand up to see the bright red blood that covered my hand. I glared at Cyrus for getting the jump on me but at the same time, I couldn't get mad at him, he wasn't at fault here.

I needed to start using more brute force if I was going to do any damage. Sidetracking myself, I looked over at Margaret for the millionth time and saw her involved with something else. I hoped she got her head out of her ass and found the cure.

I raised the sword over my head and brought it down on him but because he was taller than me, he stopped the blade with his own. He quickly slid his blade down my own and we met at the hilt of our swords. His black eyes stared into mine once again and as we held our stance, I saw a flash of red come through the black and I knew what that meant. He was fighting through her mind control. I smiled at him and winked telling him I understood what we were going to do next, I only hoped that he understood the wink.

We both bent at our elbows and shoved each other's off our swords. He flung me further across the floor than I had did with him. I quickly walked back to where I had been standing, only I ended up dragging the sword with me and my tired arm, we faced each other, and he mouthed the next part of the plan. I knew what he wanted me to do, I raised my sword and instead of aiming it at his body, I turned to Decebal, who was standing behind me, only a few feet away. Swinging my body towards her instead of facing Cyrus, I opened my mouth and tried to antagonize the person with the most power in the room. "You pissed the wrong person off, lady, didn't your mommy ever tell you not to mess with a fucking knight?" I screamed at her and brought my sword down on her head instead of Cyrus.

I wanted to slice her in two, but I didn't get the chance because once she realized what was happening, she brought her hand up and grabbed the blade before it hit her, it cut into her hand and blood began to run down her arm but she didn't let go. She met my eyes and before I could get another word of warning out, she sent an electrical current through the blade of the sword and blasted me back and away from her.

I slammed into a wall and while my body seized with the shock of the electrical current that tore through me, everything around me began to go black.

Cyrus

My mind was clouded with horrible feelings and a terrible taste in my mouth. I shook the influence she had on my mind long enough to see her send Henrietta to the wall behind us. I dropped the sword in my hand signaling to her that I was not under her influence anymore. I took no time in going over to Henrietta to see if she was alright.

I heard the witch scream behind me, but I was too concerned with how Henrietta was doing to care about what was going on over there.

I got to her side and found that her body was limp from the attack. I was not sure about what I should do, I was not acquainted with this sort of situation. I looked up to see Decebal chained to the ground and Margaret circling around her mumbling something from a book. I needed her help. "Margaret, please hurry!" I yelled to her and hoped she could spare a moment to help me with her.

She looked our way and put her book down. She hurried towards us as I gathered Henrietta into my arms. I put my ear to her chest and listened for a beat. I wasn't hearing anything beat in her chest and I knew that was not a good thing to not hear. "I do not see what your mother did to her, but she does not have a heartbeat that I can hear." Margaret ran a hand over her without touching her body, I was assuming it was to feel for a heartbeat like I had but I could not be sure, but she was not doing what I had done. "She's dead, but her soul is still intact, what I found will work. I found a spell that would break the curse, but it is very risky and extremely hard but now that she's dead, it might work better and having my mother chained to the ground will help with it as well." I was lost on what she was trying to tell me, all I could focus on was the word dead. "What is the spell, I am sure she would agree to anything at this point, just help her first." This might had been the first time I put someone else before myself and it felt right. "The spell calls for two souls to be connected together, that's how the curse gets broken and that's how I can help her. Your energy will wake her up and heal her body and her healthy state, even though she's technically dead, her previous health will allow the curse to dissipate from your system. It will also help when I kill my mother. Right now, I have her bound by magic chains, she can't do any magic while she's like this. The distraction that Henrietta made, made it possible for me to actually use the spell to bind her to the ground."

I nodded to her to go along with the plan because I would do anything right now if it meant that she would wake up. Her life was worth more than mine right now. "Okay! Lay her down flat and then you lay down next to her. Side by side. Now there may be some uncomfortable sensation during the spell but it will pass. Now, while I'm getting the spell reading I'm going to have to end my mother's life." She said it like it was not going to be a hard task for her. "Like you could ever kill me! I am a greater witch than you will ever be!" Decebal shouted from her chained to the ground stance. She was extremely upset, and I did not blame her, I hate being chained to things. I went to lay down but when I heard a horribly loud scream and then something that sounded just like the gun shot from the other day, I turned towards the witch and instead of seeing her chained to the ground she was right in front of me. Before I could do anything to stop her, her hands were around my throat and when she shoved me against the wall, hard, knocking the air out of my lungs. Her eyes narrowed in on my own and her as her teeth were bared, I waited for what she was about to do to me.

"That spell won't work if you're dead too. That knight of yours is dead and now you will be as well, I can destroy the town another way. But I'll be damned if you ended up with the happy ending." Her breath was putrid, and her words were even worse. She tightened her hand around my throat even more and when she started to whisper words that I did not understand, I began to feel something in me that I had not since I was cursed; air in my lungs.

She was taking the curse off me to kill me for good, I needed help. Now.

Before she was able to do anything, Margaret used her skills to pull her off me and then with a final word, she had the chains around her once again, only this time there was a couple new ones around her throat and torso.

Margaret walked around to face her mother head on while I laid Henrietta on the ground again, I got myself ready to lay next to her. I only hoped when she woke up that she was not angry at me for agreeing to use magic on her. "You see, Mother, I don't have to be a better witch than you, I just have to pin you down in one place, take the knife in my hand, and then stab you right in the heart. Because in the end, you are just a human that can use magic." I watched Margaret speak to her mother and then raise the knife she had in her hand above her head and then she shoved it down into her chest.

The second she ran her mother through, I felt the weight of her death come off my chest. I could feel the curse moving through my body, it was restless, and it wanted out. The rest was up to Margaret. I watched her clean her hands off and drop the knife on the ground, not before she wiped the blood from the knife onto her hand to use later. She grabbed a book and walked towards us. "Lay back down, this will take a minute or two. I need you to be as still as she is right now. Movement will only make it take longer. I have to create a bridge between your two souls after all." When she spoke about the soul bridge or whatever, I was a bit worried that it was not going to go well, but I had no other options and neither did Henrietta.

I laid still for what seemed like forever until I heard her start talking again. "I call upon the elders of magic itself to bring these two souls and make them as one. Take the curse from one and the limited life source from the other and seal their souls together. Create a bridge so that one shall heal and the other shall be cleansed of any evil placed on them. Let this last for eternity, giving them a never-ending life."

I heard the last part of the request and I nearly asked about it before the searing pain struck my chest and mind. It was absolute torture and I could barely hear what Margaret was saying anymore. My hearing was going in and out, and the pain was even worse. She said it would not last long, but I think she was absolutely wrong.

I felt the heat of the pain for a moment longer when it began to die out of my system. I had closed my eyes before the pain started and when I opened them again, I saw the world in a much different way. The room seemed bigger for one, and my senses were completely changed. I could smell things I had never before and my hearing, it was so tuned that I could hear the heartbeat of Henrietta next to me.

The thought of her heart beating faster made mine swell. I turned my head and looked over at her. She laid there with her battle armor on and her hair falling around her head like a beautiful gray halo of hair. Her face was quiet and her breathing even. I watched as Margaret walked over to see my face up close. "It worked, you should see yourself, your highness." She used a proper greeting and it sounded odd coming from her. Never the less, I started to stand up.

The first thing I noticed was that my body felt different, I was not tired constantly and I did not have memories playing in my head at all times. I lifted my hand to my face and saw that my skin was smooth again, like it had been before. I felt the contours of my face and felt that they were the same as my arms and hands. I was brought out of my amazement when I heard Henrietta take in a deep breath and then start to cough it up.

I rushed down to her and helped her into a sitting position. Her eyes slowly opened and when they met mine, she gasped. "Cyrus, what the hell happened?" I was not sure if she was angry or surprised. "Margaret did it, she lifted the curse. Everything is back to the way it was right before I was cursed, I'm back to my old age, well young age, aside from the year and the people around me, it is like I was never cursed." Her eyes would not stop staring at me. I was not aware that I was much to look at.

Her look of wonder and astonishment made me smile, I did not want to admit it to myself before because I could not fathom the possibility, but I believed I was falling in love with this amazing woman.

She took her eyes off me for a moment so that Margaret could explain what she did. I, however, did not do the same; I took my time and kept note of her face while she spoke with Margaret. "So, the whole eternity thing, does that mean he and I can't die? Like we're immortal?" Her question was one I had been thinking about as well. I had lived for so long that an eternity did not seem like something I would like, maybe if it was with her. "That was the big catch when I bridged your souls together, the only way that it would have worked would have been to make you two immortals as well. It's not like a vampire thing unless you want to think of it as such, it's more like you have to live forever, you can't die." Henrietta sat back on her butt and got lost in a thought. "But if we ever wanted to die, could we? Like if we lived for a good thousand years and we got bored of life or tired of living, could we end our own lives?" That was a good question. "You would both have to die at the same time and in the same way, plus you would need my help, or a stronger witch to take it off. It would be the only way your souls would be allowed to go to their after lives." She shrugged and stared at the both of us. "Henrietta, I know this is a lot to take in, but if she had not have done what she did, you would have stayed dead. Now I know we have not known each other long but would you care to spend the rest of eternity together?" It was a bold question I knew, but it had to be said. "Well I–I'm not sure, I thought about a whole lot of ways, this could have turned out in the end but living for the rest of eternity was not one of them. But I think I could make it work, I mean I've missed enough school, who needs an education when I could learn things from around the world for the rest of my life? And spending it with you would be a great adventure." Her words touched my heart and I knew she meant them because she looked at me the same way she had since she first started getting along with me, before I was curse free.

I looked around the castle walls and saw everything that was wrong with it. "I guess we have some cleaning up to do, this place is filthy." I heard a laugh next to me and when I looked over to her, I saw her face light up with a smile and her bright beautiful brown eyes looking back at me like I was the only thing on her mind.

"Well, we have the rest of eternity to do so, let's get started." She stood up and dusted herself off and reached for my hand. We stood together for a moment, but that was killed the second we heard the grinding sound of rocks beginning to fall away from each other.

"The castle is falling down." Henrietta's voice touched my ears and when I looked up, I started to see the outside light coming through the cracks quicker and quicker.

"We need to leave. Now."

With our hands intertwined, we ran out of the castle with Margaret on our heels and the last of the castle falling behind us. What a way to start an eternity together.

CPSIA information can be obtained
at www.ICGtesting.com
Printed in the USA
LVHW020525040121
675399LV00005B/549